NIGHTFALL IN CAIRO

Ezzedine C. Fishere

Translated from Arabic by the author

Edited by Sharidan Russell

Commonsense House

First edition published by Commonsense House
Hanover, New Hampshire, in February 2026

Original title, *Kul Hādhā al-Hurā'a*, published By Dar El Karma in
Cairo, January 2017

ISBN: 979 8 9946532 1 0

"Shitty days are good for bed."

An Egyptian proverb

CONTENTS

A Promise

It began with a call from an unknown number. Early summer, the term dragging, the air heavy with dust. I was bored—that's the only reason I answered.

He said his name was Omar. Nothing, until: "I'm the son of your friend Fakhreddine." Oh. *That* Omar. It had been years since I'd heard the name. He wanted to meet. "Tomorrow," he said. His voice carried a genuine urgency. I knew his father well, knew his background story, so I said yes.

We met in a café near campus. He was already at a corner table, sitting forward, elbows on the wood. No coffee, no water. He didn't bother with hello. Instead, he reached into his bag and slid a USB across the table with the tips of his fingers.

"It's an audio file," he said. "Stories I recorded with Amal Mofeed." He didn't look up when he said her name. Whether she was a friend, or a lover…he didn't say. "Maybe turn it into a novel," he added, quieter, as if unsure it was reasonable.

I wasn't looking for a project. Everyone thinks their story should be published; most shouldn't. But I was bored, and I have a weakness for the unguarded certainty of the young. I remembered when no one cared about my stories. I told him I'd give it a shot. He kept his eyes on the USB, like it might shift under its own power, then stood abruptly.

"Thank you," he said quickly and walked out.

Driving home, I pressed play. His voice—low, deliberate—unfolded the story. Hers cut in, bright and certain, the pronounced American accent hitting my ear like cold water. Outside, Cairo traffic blared and seethed, but I stayed with them. The city thinned away. I carried the voices upstairs, let them pour into the dark, and listened until the last word. Just before midnight.

The next morning, we met again. Same café, same corner. He was more jittery this time, bouncing his knee under the table. I told him I liked the stories. I wanted to publish them. "Minimal edits," I said. "Just enough to stitch the background and fill the silences."

He blinked, sat back.

"I didn't think you would. It's Amal who pushed me."

"They're good stories."

A shrug, eyes on the floor.

"Why would anyone care?"

That question!

"I don't know, Omar" I said. "But if we all waited for guarantees, nothing would ever get published. Worst case, it flops. No one reads it. Life goes on."

Reluctantly, he agreed, still avoiding my eyes.

Over the summer, we met a few more times. I asked for what was missing—the details, the feelings, the spaces between words. Sometimes he'd give me a half-smile before answering, as if he were deciding what to hold back.

Then came the problem of modesty.

Not long before, a writer had been jailed because a reader claimed offense to his modesty. I told Omar: these stories are bold. People will be offended. He gave that same half-smile.

"Are you ready to go to jail for this?"

A puzzled look.

"Why would I? Your name's on the cover."

"But it's your story," I said. "I'm just the messenger."

We asked around—friends, publishers, lawyers. The answer was the same: if certain people want you in jail, you'll go. The law isn't the point. Approval? No. Publish abroad? Won't help—you're here.

Omar leaned back in his chair, crossed his arms. "Up to you," he said.

I chose to publish, but with this warning: if you're worried about your modesty, don't read the fucking book. No one is forcing you. You pick it up, you open it, you keep turning the pages—that's on you. So, if you do, then take offense and drag us into court, lock one or both of us up, I'll write another book. About you.

And I will not be kind.

And its memory will outlast you.

This is a promise.

Ezzedine Fishere.

1

Amal and Omar
Wake Up

Friday, 9 a.m.

"You awake?"

She didn't reply. He watched the slow rise of her back, the spill of black hair across her shoulders—thick, heavy, disordered. He wondered, briefly, if it was natural or chemically smoothed. A pointless thought. He reached out, brushed his fingers through it. His hand continued down the curve of her spine, over the swell of her hip. Her body felt denser now, more than it had in the half-light of night. His gaze followed her leg, her ankle, the pale arch of her foot.

Suddenly, she turned:

"You taking pictures?"

He was more surprised by her American accent than embarrassed by the question. He met her question with a shrug, eyes steady.

"I thought about grabbing the camera but got lazy."

"Thank God."

"How long have you been awake?"

"Since you started staring."

She rolled toward him. Their faces aligned. A brush of noses, half a smile, then a whisper of a kiss—so light it barely touched his lips. He smiled awkwardly and kissed her again, deeper this time. She kissed him back, slow and deliberate. Deeper still. She turned onto her side, facing him. He shifted closer, lips finding her cheek, her neck, the slope of her back. She touched his penis, feeling his erection, then drew him inside her. Eye to eye, they moved together until they came, again, as they had at dawn.

***

Noon.

"You awake?"

He didn't reply. She studied his back, his skin the shade of burnt sugar, the short black curls, the slight twist of his arm, the muscles. She reached toward his chest, then stopped. A hand half-raised, like reaching for chocolate and remembering the diet. He's so young, she thought. Christ!

She shook her head and slid from the bed. Hunger gnawed at her. Last night had taken more out of her than expected. She rarely drank, not like that. But the second glass had dissolved her restraint. Five followed. Or six. It had begun with wine, then a cocktail. Then toasts. And then...whatever that was. She'd nearly blacked out, hadn't drunk that much since high school prom. But unlike prom, this time she'd woken next to someone she knew, or almost knew.

She moved to the kitchen, put bread in the toaster and turned on the coffeemaker. The fridge was full, absurdly so. Her friend had stocked it. She hadn't seen food like this in five years. Her jail time had been mostly solitary, gray, with rationed food. One egg, not a carton. Milk in sachets. Feta cheese, always. Tomatoes were rare. Cucumbers, watery and limp. Certainly no avocados, or smoked salmon, or peanut butter. The lettuce wasn't this green. Now here they were, all these little treasures. She touched them, one by one, gently. Her eyes were hungry for everything, but her stomach wasn't ready yet. Five days ago, when she was released, she'd tried to eat real food, but everything came up. So she went back to the prison menu: bread, feta cheese, and cucumber. That would do for now.

She sliced a cucumber, poured hot water, arranged the tray like a ceremony. She returned to the bedroom. Omar appeared to be deeply asleep, but he suddenly turned, his eyes open, brown, alert, inscrutable.

"That for both of us or just you?"

She met his gaze. There was something in it. Defensiveness? A challenge? She answered, her voice tight:

"It's for both of us."

"Thanks."

He reached for the tray, but she didn't pass it to him.

"I don't like eating in bed."

"Ok. Got a table?"

"Two: kitchen or living room."

"Either's fine."

"How flexible!" she said. "Follow me."

She walked into the living room thinking about his tone. Dry. Sardonic. That was how she remembered him from the handful of times they'd crossed paths. It used to make her laugh. Maybe it even drew her in, a little, back then, but she wasn't sure now. She didn't usually go for men who were so rough around the edges. Although with him it was oddly ornamental, like a chipped vase. It was a performed detachment, the kind that masked neither cruelty nor crassness. Just rough texture, possibly from lack of use. He was, what, twenty-one?

"How old are you?" she asked.

"Why?"

"You drove me in a taxi, didn't you? So you must be older than twenty-one."

"Who said I had a license?"

"Great. So how old are you really?"

"Why? Are you worried they'll accuse you of corrupting a minor? Don't worry. They can't send you back to jail now."

"Oh. So you know."

"I was at your party, remember? Anyway, all of Egypt knows. You're a star."

"Wonderful. Do they know what I look like too?"

"Not really. Maybe the ones who followed the trial. Most just know the name from the headlines."

"But you know the name and the face."

"Of course. We've met before. Three times."

"I thought so. Didn't we talk about this last night at the party? Before you took me home for the...finale?"

"So, you *do* remember."

"Flashes. I remember the end of the party, or my end of it. But some of it is hazy...a moment in the cab, me trying to get out. Then black. Then...I do remember the other things. So—how old?"

"Twenty-two."

"Jesus. Seven years younger!"

He didn't answer, so she pressed on,

"Why were you driving a cab? You're not a cab driver!"

"I told you last night."

"I think I blacked out before that part."

He raised an eyebrow, "You mean before the vomiting?"

"Sorry! Did I ruin the car seat?"

"No, not entirely. But you definitely left your mark!"

"Ha. Does this happen often to you?"

"Which part? The puking or the...sequel?"

"Both," she pressed.

"Not really."

"Which one?"

"Both."

"Good. Glad to be on the short list. Just don't call me Auntie Amal."

"When's your flight?"

"Tomorrow night. After midnight. That's the table, by the way, in case you didn't notice."

"Cut the sarcasm."

He placed the tray on the table and sat down. She reached for her plate and began eating. He waited a bit, then followed. She glanced at the single tomato left on the tray, then at him. A silent offer.

"Can we shift to Arabic?" he asked.

"I don't know Arabic."

"Really? Not even a word?"

"Not enough. Your English is fine. Let's split the tomato."

"I'm done; you eat it. Got any cigarettes?"

She shook her head. He looked around, restless.

"How badly do you want to smoke? On a scale of one to ten?"

"Ten."

She tilted her head, considered, then got up, found her phone, and dialed. She asked what brand he wanted and ordered it, then sat back down, expressionless.

"I don't allow smoking in here. But I'll make an exception."

"I'm so grateful."

"Seven years younger...my God."

She cleared the tray and walked to the kitchen. He stayed by the window, unsure of what to do next. He watched her disappear down the hall. The bathroom door closed, locked behind her. Why lock it? He heard her start the shower and sat in silence. The doorbell rang. She emerged in a white robe, took the pack from the delivery guy, tossed it at Omar, and vanished again. He lit a cigarette at the window. He still couldn't believe any of this. He was sitting in his boxer briefs, in this fancy apartment, smoking at this beautiful woman's window while she showered. *How did this happen?* It felt like an out of body experience: the whole night he had been watching himself, watching both of them together as if it weren't quite real. As if they were cast in a movie scene. Even now, he felt like he could see himself in a scene that he couldn't leave. His entire life was a series of scenes. And he often ended up in the middle of things, but he never knew what to do. As though he were in a scene, but nobody gave him the script, so he never knew his lines. In the end, he usually didn't do much. He would just watch, indecisive. Should he get dressed and walk out or stick around? He'd asked his friends once about this paralysis. 'Do what feels right,' was all they said. He scoffed, nothing ever felt quite right.

She reappeared, wearing a loose, thigh-length white shirt. Her brown skin was luminous under the white fabric. The shirt lifted slightly as she walked. She didn't fidget with the hem. Didn't hide. He wondered how she moved so comfortably in her body, how she didn't flinch at his direct gaze. Last night, he was taken by her ease in bed, the comfort with which her body yielded to his touch, her hands exploring his body, pulling him closer to her, taking him in, pressing against him. Her mouth, her hands, her body—open, unafraid. Every part of her touched every part of him, wrapping herself around him like a second skin, eyes wide open, looking into his, drinking him in. He'd never seen anything like it. He assumed it was the effect of the alcohol, but now she was sober. He hadn't been with many women. The few he had been with were experienced, one was a professional, but he had never been with someone like Amal. She was at peace with herself, with him, with what they did together. She took him like she was sipping water, savoring it slowly, without a hint of inhibition. She stopped beside him.

"So," she said carefully. "What do you want to do now?"

Ah. That question. He felt awkward. Should he have left right after the cigarette? Or after breakfast? Or even earlier; should he have slipped out in the morning and vanished before they were both awake and sober? Who had made that rule? Billy Crystal in *When Harry Met Sally*. Sally had called it a jerk move, but she'd been in love with Harry, even though she didn't know it yet. So, Harry was probably right: if it's not love, leave early. He wasn't in love. They'd only met a few times. But he didn't want to leave. Something about her held him, unlocked some knot inside him. Maybe he wanted to be like that, too?

"Hello?"

"Sorry. I zoned out," he said. "I'm not sure what I'll do today. Probably run errands for Aunt Layla. She's not really my aunt—she's my dad's cousin. But I call her 'Aunt.'"

"It's okay."

"I should go," he said, then hesitated. "Need help with anything? Dishes or something?"

"No need."

"You're flying out tomorrow, right?"

"Yes. After midnight."

"You must have a million things to do. Sorry if I've delayed you."

She smiled, a half-smile, like someone entertaining a child.

"Delayed me?"

She set her coffee cup down. Walked toward him, slowly. She stood close without touching him. He tensed, slightly. She moved her head closer to his until her lips met his. A long kiss, silent. Then she pulled away, her voice calm:

"Thanks for the delay. It was the best thing I've done all week."

He smiled, unsure. She didn't smile back, just went to her chair and picked up her cup again.

"The truth is," she said, "I've done everything I needed to do. Nothing left for me but to go to the airport."

"Really?"

"Yep. Suitcase packed. My friends insisted on helping. They even cleaned. I'm all set."

"You don't want to go out? See anyone?"

"I've seen everyone. Multiple times. Last night was the grand finale."

"Family?"

"The ones who matter couldn't make it to Cairo in time. The ones who live here don't want to be seen with me."

"So, how will you go to the airport?"

"Why, looking for cab fare?"

He shrugged. She looked at him intently.

"Stay," she said. "Stay with me until tomorrow night. Then take me to the airport."

He hesitated. "Sure. Or I could leave now and come back tomorrow to drive you."

"Or you could stay and not drive me. Or leave and not come back. Or jump off the balcony. The possibilities are endless. I'm not asking to think through the options, young man, I'm asking if you'll stay. Do you understand the question?"

"Yes."

"Then why don't you answer it?"

"Okay."

"How generous. What is this—pity? Fresh-out-of-prison compassion?"

"No, not at all."

"So, do you want to stay with me for this last weekend or

not? Answer clearly."

"I'd be happy to stay. No need to get hysterical."

"Good, then say it clearly."

"I just did. I'd be glad to stay. I'd be glad to spend the weekend with you. But why do you want to spend your last weekend in Cairo with me?"

She went quiet for a while, then said slowly:

"Because I don't want to be alone. I've spent five years with only my own company And I'm tired of it."

"Why not invite some of your friends back? That party had over a hundred people."

"I can't handle any more noise. Not in my current state. Listening to more than one person exhausts me. Maybe it is the impact of prison's quietness. Like my stomach and food. Or maybe the past few days just wore me out. But frankly, I kind of miss the prison routine. The stillness."

"You don't want to—"

She continued, not hearing him:

"And I don't want to be with someone I know, someone with whom I have history. I don't want complications. No affection, no jealousy, no worry. Not today. You're actually perfect for the job. Someone I barely know, just enough to trust you. And you know almost nothing about me, just what the media said. Like two people meeting on a train. A one-night stand extended into a weekend. Just quiet company to pass these 36 hours. That's all. Deal?"

"Deal."

"And we're off to a good start."

She smiled. Then it faded, quickly, as she slipped back into thought.

"A very good start.," he said.

"But—I do have some conditions."

"Ah. Here we go."

"I want you to tell me stories. About these years while I was in prison."

"You didn't follow the news?"

"I don't want the news. I want stories. Real people stories."

"And you'll tell yours too?"

"No. You talk, I listen."

"And why would I agree to be your Scheherazade? What's in it for me?"

"What's in it for you? Really? A weekend with me! How many times do you get to spend two days with a woman like me?"

He paused, so she went on:

"I'll take that as a yes. And one more rule: we're totally honest. No filters."

"And why is that?"

"Because I say so. Because I'm leaving and won't be back for a long time. Because I just got out of prison and need to speak honestly, like I'm thinking out loud. I want to hear real thoughts."

"Fine."

"Are you sure?"

"Why not? How often do I get to spend two days with a woman like you?"

"I like the sarcasm."

She set her cup down again. Her voice dropped.

"And since we're being honest—why don't we go back to bed, take off these clothes, and pick up where we left off this morning?"

***

2 p.m.

"Awake?"

"Yeah."

"Can we speak Arabic?"

"Again? I told you that I don't speak Arabic. I wish I did, but I don't. Clear enough?"

"Clear."

"And your English is excellent, so stop bringing this up. Where'd you learn it anyway?"

"Online."

"Excuse me?"

"The Internet."

"How?"

"I'll tell you. But first, I want you to tell me your story."

"You already know my story, from the media."

"I mean before prison. What brought you to Cairo, and so on?"

"I thought we agreed you would tell the stories?"

"Consider it a down payment. A gesture to encourage your Scheherazade."

"Are you always bargaining like this? Fine. I was born in Cairo — in Shubra actually. My father, Ahmed Mofeed, was an army officer. He went on several missions to the States and retired as a brigadier general. Then he moved us to Washington and started a business trading in military equipment. I was six then."

"Wait! Your dad is an arms dealer?"

"No. He facilitated deals in communication systems and other military tech I barely understand. It was sometimes weapons-related, sometimes civilian related. Anyway, his business was successful. We weren't rich, but we lived well, had a nice home in Virginia. Then my dad died while I was in college, and we stayed on."

"And your mom?"

"A professional assassin. Kidding. She helped with his business, took over for a while after he died, then sold the company, put the money in safe investments, and opened a flower shop."

"From arms to flowers?"

"I told you it wasn't arms. Communication systems."

"Right."

"After college, I felt lost. My father was gone; my mom and sister were absorbed in their own worlds. I had a degree in history, but no idea what to do with it, or even who I was. I mean, I knew my parents were from Egypt, but I felt completely American. I didn't speak Arabic, didn't go to weekend Arabic schools, didn't spend evenings watching old Egyptian movies with my family. My memories of Egypt were limited to brief, chaotic summer visits. In my mind, I was just another American girl. But after 9/11, my name—and all the hysteria that followed—forced the identity question on me. I suddenly became 'different' in a way that seemed to make a lot of people uncomfortable. What surprised me the most was that other Arab-American girls also found me 'different.' Those who'd learned Arabic, taken religion classes, were raised to believe their values made them superior to the 'Americans,' those who didn't party, didn't drink, didn't have sex—they made me feel I wasn't different enough, or that I was some kind of a lost soul."

"And where did you end up between these two sides?"

"Honestly, I got crushed in the middle. Sometimes I found comfort in leaning into the Arab side. I would try learning Arabic, pray, stop drinking, all that. Then, at other times, I swung the other way completely, so far that my 'Arab' friends cut me off. In their eyes, or at least their mothers', I was a *sharmoota*—that is the first Arabic word I learnt. Ultimately, I went back to school to escape all that. I left Virginia, left all our family friends and school connections, and moved to California to study law. I passed the bar exam at twenty-four."

"Not bad."

"Not at all. Maybe I was a *sharmoota*, but I wasn't stupid. After graduation, I got offers from big law firms, but I wanted more than just a big paycheck. I wanted to do something meaningful. Like I said, we weren't rich, but we had enough. I didn't want to waste my life chasing more. And after watching my dad die suddenly, I realized that nothing lasts. Whatever time I had, I didn't want to spend it doing things I hated. I joined an NGO working in development. The pay was crap, but I was hooked. Travel to Africa, Asia, South America. Dozens of projects changing people's lives."

"Changing lives?"

"Yes. Not the life of everyone, but enough. I saw kids go to schools we built, women find livelihoods they wouldn't have had otherwise, ex-fighters learn something to do after war besides killing, clean water reach villages for the first time, young people start small businesses with a few dollars. It wasn't perfect, the organization had issues for sure, but despite all the crap, that work gave me a reason to wake up every morning."

"So, why'd you leave it?"

"Because: Egypt called me!"

"How did Egypt get your number?"

"Don't mock me. I'm serious. I asked myself why not do this work in Egypt, where I had family roots? I thought it might be a chance to resolve the identity issue for good. I also thought I'd be more effective here. Naively, I believed that because I had ties to Egypt, people would accept me more easily than they would a white American or European. I ignored my colleagues' warnings. They told me that people in developing countries often prefer foreigners who look nothing like them over foreigners who seem familiar. I told them Egypt was different. I repeated all the lines I'd heard from my friends' parents: Egyptian kinship, warmth, kindness...all that nonsense. My boss looked at me with pity. I gave her the same look. And since the organization didn't operate in the Arab world, I quit and joined one that did."

"The one behind the conspiracy?"

"What conspiracy?"

"To divide Egypt and topple the state?"

"Ah yes, that one. What was it called again? 'The International Teddy Bear Organization?' Yes, the job vacancy even said it: 'State-topplers wanted. No experience required.'"

"No, seriously, how did you find that job? I never understand how people get those gigs."

"There are dozens of American organizations working in development all over the world. If you've graduated from a decent school, it's easy to get in. With my experience, I had several offers. I was about to accept one, similar to my previous job, but then I talked to my mom."

"Your mom? plot twist."

"Yeah, she popped up out of nowhere, really. She's not the meddling type. Even when I ask for her opinion, she usually flips the question back to me. That's her parenting style. I'm not complaining, it works for me. I can't imagine having a mom who interferes in my business. Anyway, she suddenly had all these questions about what I was doing—me, a lawyer, working in foreign aid. She asked if my contributions to clean water projects were a good use of my skills. She asked about the impact of these projects in a country like Egypt. 'How many schools will you build in five years? How many wells will you dig? And what does that matter compared to what the Egyptian government spends on these sectors?' I gave her the standard answers—individual action matters, we can't just wait on the government. She didn't argue, but she said that if I could improve government performance by even one-thousandth of a percent, the impact would be hundreds of times greater than all the schools and wells we'd build in five years."

"So, your mom was the instigator? The mastermind of the conspiracy?"

"Pretty much. Don't forget, my mom is the real Egyptian in this story. Born and raised in Shubra. When it was about Costa Rica or Lesotho, she let her daughter play. But when it came to Egypt, she had opinions. She said, 'What wells are you going to dig, girl? Egypt doesn't need more holes. Go fill the ones already swallowing the country's money.' When I asked how I was supposed to fix the holes of corruption, she said all Egyptians know the answer, but they lack the means and the hope to do it. What people like me can offer is to give them that hope and those means. In two sentences, my flower-selling mother summed up a global theory of civic politics. She was so clear, so persuasive. I got the point immediately. A week later, I started a job with an organization that worked on strengthening civil society. Two months later, I landed in Cairo."

"January 2010?"

"Bravo. You really did your homework."

"Not really. But the media latched onto that date as proof of your role in the international conspiracy to divide Egypt and bring down the state. You're an American citizen who previously lived in Turkey, visited Doha twice and Tehran once—you hit all the usual centers of conspiracy. You only missed Tel Aviv. One commentator even said, 'Ask yourself:

why did she arrive in January? Why January of all months? And is it just coincidence that three weeks later protests break out?'"

She laughed. "The *real* joke is that investigators asked me that exact question. Ten times, at least. They asked about my 'assignments,' what I brought in my luggage, whether it contained advanced communication equipment."

"And you confessed!"

"Of course I did. I told them my job was to strengthen civil society organizations, help them expose corruption, articulate public demands, formulate policies, and pressure the government to adopt them. That's what my job letter said. Naturally, I spoke with protesters. I was in Tahrir from January 28 to the end. Naturally, I gave food to hungry protesters and cash to others to buy water and sandwiches. They were thrilled with these 'confessions.' I asked where, exactly, I had broken the law. Is protesting illegal for Egyptians? Is feeding or hydrating sit-in participants a crime? They smiled and closed the file."

"So you're a conspirator and proud of it."

"#ProudConspirator. I worked with hundreds of organizations, maybe thousands of people, many of them government employees. They attended trainings, workshops, participated in events. Where were the authorities then? Where was the outrage when we met with officials? When we applied—over and over—to legalize our status, why did they tell us to 'go ahead and work until the law is amended?' Anyway, I won't reargue the case. Let's have a drink."

"Before that, I need to confess something."

"Go ahead."

"The workshops I attended with your center..."

"What about them?"

"My participation didn't really mean anything."

"What do you mean?"

"I only went because my girlfriend at the time pushed me. She said I'd benefit. But I wasn't in a position or job that needed that kind of training."

"How many workshops did you come to?"

"Three."

"Ah, right. Those are the three times we met. And how did we even let you in?"

"I claimed the company I worked for had a project related to the workshop. The truth is, I did benefit, but only personally. No one else gained from what I learned. Sorry."

"Don't be. Honestly, half the participants don't use what they learn directly. When we design these workshops, we assume at least half won't apply the knowledge now, but they might one day, when they finally get off their ass and engage."

"Great. So they'll never use it."

"They will. You might not see it now, but the day will come."

"Wow. Your name really suits your optimism, *Amal*."

"You know how many people have already made that joke?"

"Sorry. But seriously, there's no hope. Let's not pretend. Maybe there was a window during the Tahrir days, but that's long gone."

"Dear God."

"What? Do you disagree?

"Of course I do. This is all temporary. It'll pass."

"Yeah, when I'm seventy! By then, I won't just have forgotten what I learned in those workshops, I'll have forgotten who I am."

"You don't forget who you are at seventy! Don't worry. You have time."

"Maybe. If I don't wind up disappeared or dead by then. You, meanwhile, will be back in America. Now, can you please get up and make us coffee or do something useful?"

"You get up. Come, I'll show you how to make your own damn coffee."

He sat, again, on the windowsill, the coffee cup beside him cooling slowly. Across from him, Amal sat cross-legged in the armchair, watching him in that calm, unapologetic way of hers. Every time she lifted the cup to her mouth, her shirt lifted slightly too, just enough to reveal the curved line of her hip.

He tried not to stare.

Why is there no pleasant Arabic word for a woman's hips? The dictionary coughed up its usual offerings: *ist, dubur, ridf, safila, maq'ada, wara', mo'akhkhera*, all of which sound like anatomical warnings. And of course, there is the word everyone thinks of but never says. All ugly names for something so beautiful. So unfair to the hips. What was he supposed to say? How could he tell a woman that he loved that part of her body without sounding crass or anatomical? Should he point vaguely to her hips and mumble something like 'this is nice?'

And what about pussy? The dictionary was equally stern and anatomical. *Mihbal,* it insisted, is the inside. *Farj,* the outside. As if they were rooms in a house no one named. The vulgar name, *kuss,* the dictionary noted grimly, wasn't even Arabic. Probably Turkish or Persian. In English—thank God for English—it was easier. But in those moments, the intimate ones, English vanished for him. It wasn't the language he reached for when touching her skin breathlessly. So, what could he say? 'Your *mihbal* is beautiful?' 'I love copulating with you?'

How can a language spoken by 400 million people have no decent words for body parts they touch daily, or for acts they, one would hope, engage in regularly? As if some higher power sexually muted Arabs. They touch and see these parts, perform these acts, but say nothing about it. Not a word. What deeper repression could there be?

She moved.

He looked up.

"You want more coffee?" he asked

She shook her head, scratched the skin just above the part no one named, then reached for a cigarette.

"I thought you didn't smoke?"

"They're my cigarettes, remember?"

"Just asking."

"Come on, tell your story," she insisted.

"No, it's still your turn. Finish yours."

"The rest is boring."

"Fine, summarize if you like."

"Why? Getting bored?"

"Just tell it already."

"The media already told the whole thing. Five years ago, they raided a bunch of civil society organizations—ours included. They shut us down, confiscated our papers, our computers, and took anyone they found in the office. They charged us with that foreign funding case. You know the rest. Some people fled. I stayed. I didn't want to leave."

"Out of patriotism? Or stubbornness?"

"Neither. Probably guilt. Maybe the identity issue again. I didn't want to be one of those who riles people up then vanishes when things get tough. I refused to play the foreigner, the protected. I wanted to stay with the others."

He looked at her silently.

"I know what you're thinking. Sure, I had some sense of safety, drawn from my American citizenship and from our organization's connections in D.C. I knew the U.S. government couldn't drop the case, even if it wanted to. The media, my friends and colleagues, wouldn't let them. But that was just part of it. I also believed being imprisoned alongside others might actually help them. That I'd be a kind of shield."

"And then?"

"Then I got tired. Five years is a long time. And prison is a miserable place. I was worn out. I wanted out. I needed a break."

"What about the others?"

"Well, it turned out I'd miscalculated. The Egyptian authorities no longer feared imprisoning American citizens. Or maybe they did a little, but not enough to stop. Me staying in prison meant nothing, didn't help the case or the others."

"But you got out before your sentence was over."

"Yep, that's the deal. But I had to give up my Egyptian citizenship."

"That's what upset you?"

"In part."

"Come on. Ditching Egyptian citizenship is the best part of the deal. If I were you, I'd burn my Egyptian passport right at the airport. It's a curse, not a nationality. Nationality is supposed to give you rights. This one only deprives you of them."

"Dear God!" she scoffed.

"Think about it. This citizenship is practically a certificate of enslavement. Just having it loads you with obligations and takes away your rights. If you were Colombian-American, would you have been shamed like you were during the trial? Called a traitor, a whore of the West? Never. But just being Egyptian gives a hundred million strangers a claim on you, a right to judge you by standards that apply only to their own. Even entering Egypt is easier for foreigners—no one stops *them* at the airport. Renting an apartment? Easier. No broker or landlord questions your morals or treats you like a slut because you're living on your own. Even hiring a cleaner is easier for a foreigner. Taxi drivers take you where you want, no haggling. Cops leave you alone. If they do arrest you, they'll spare you the beatings and insults. You can party, drink, kiss your partner in public, wear rags or couture, eat street food or dine at five-star places. Everyone treats you with respect. Want to have a glass of beer in Ramadan? Only if you're not Egyptian! Even the snobbish Gezira Club opens its doors for foreigners, just because they have a different passport. So why the hell would anyone keep Egyptian citizenship if they had another?"

"Because it's part of who I am, you jerk! And I won't let anyone strip it from me. And just so you know, I'll start the process of claiming my Egyptian citizenship back as soon as my case is settled in the US. And if the consulate refuses to give me a passport, I'll sue them—all the way to the highest court."

"You clearly have time on your hands."

"Don't say stupid things."

"Relax. Just answer me this: does this citizenship give you anything besides restrictions, in Egypt or abroad?"

"Listen, don't pull the 'authentic Egyptian' card with me. I'm sick of being treated like the foreigner. I'm not one—not here, not in America. You and people like you don't have deeper insight into the country just because you're ignorant of anything outside it. I've lived in multiple cultures. That lets me see each one more clearly—or at least it means I'm not clueless, or in need of some translator-guide to explain things to me. Got it?"

"Alright, alright. Calm down."

"I came here in 2010. That year was hell. Everything and everyone I met here shocked me. If I hadn't needed to keep working to pay off my student loan, and if I wasn't afraid of failing in the eyes of my mom, I'd have left within two months. All the things you say don't happen to foreigners did happen to me, and worse. Sure, people treat foreigners well. But once they hear my name is Amal, that's it. They revoke all the privileges and treat me like a failed Egyptian, which is worse. First question I get: 'Are you Muslim?' Once I say yes, the gates of hell open: 'Where are your parents? Your husband? Why are you dressed like that? Why do you go to these places? Why stay out late? Why do you laugh like that? Why do you drink? Why don't you pray? Why don't you learn Arabic? Why do you dance like that? Do you have sex? Don't you fear God?' Constant judgment, constant guilt. I've always felt like a kind, loving, warm person—and that's how I've been treated everywhere. Except by Arabs, here and in America. They're the only ones who've only ever made me feel dirty…a slut, *sharmoota!*"

"I rest my case. Then why did you stay? And why do you want to keep that cursed citizenship now?"

"Because everything had changed in 2011. A revolution happened. 2011 was the best year of my life. Suddenly, my nationality didn't matter. I was American and was loved by Egyptians. For a change nobody taunted me for the U.S. support for Israel or the invasion of Iraq as if I were personally running American foreign policy. That year, people were kind, hopeful, generous. I felt powerful in a way I never had before."

"2011 was long time ago."

"I am aware of that. But that doesn't mean I give up my rights. Citizenship gives me rights, even if people and governments ignore them. And I won't surrender them. I will fight for my Egyptian rights, and for my American rights. And

I'll hold onto my faith, as I see it—not how others want me to live it."

"*Egypt will always be dear to me,*" Omar sang sarcastically.

"Go make more coffee."

"Alright. But finish the story."

"That's it. I surrendered the passport; they released me as if they were deporting me to serve the rest of my sentence in the US. I got out five days ago. I wrapped up the paperwork and travel prep. My friend threw me this party to say goodbye. She invited everyone, literally, even you, whose name I barely remembered. The rest you know."

"There's more."

"More?"

"The part I don't know. What did you do in those years in Egypt before jail, besides wrestling with your identity and conspiring? Did you fall in love? Did something shift in how you see Egypt or yourself? Anything?"

"Coffee first."

"Alright. Coffee then."

He got up and walked out.

"Shut the door behind you."

"Why?"

"Just do it."

"Okay."

***

He came back to bed with the coffee and handed her the cup. She set it on the sheets and leaned against the wall, stretching her legs out in front of her. There was no room left for him on the bed. He hesitated, then sat on the chair facing her. She sipped in silence. He did the same.

"This mattress kills my back," she complained

"Isn't this your own bed?"

"It is. But I haven't slept on it in a long time. I'm not sure if the mattress has stiffened or my back just got used to the prison cot."

"What'll happen to the apartment when you leave? How has it stayed empty all this time?"

"The organization paid the rent. They refused to let anyone else move in as a political statement. It doesn't matter. I think they'll keep it for a few weeks, let whoever's replacing me see it, and decide whether to keep it or not. Why? Looking for a place?"

"No. Just curious."

"There's no such thing as 'just curious.' Every question wants something."

They both went quiet. He looked at her shiny brown legs, slightly fuller at the thighs, narrowing at the waist, then her body widening again up to her shoulders—an hourglass.

"Stop staring."

"Why?"

"I don't know. Your look is bothering me."

"It didn't bother you before."

"You're right. Sorry. It's probably my body that bothers me."

"Why?"

"Because it's not the body I know. It's changed."

"It doesn't look different from last time."

"Then you clearly weren't paying attention. It got flabbier this past year. I tried to control it—food, exercise—but the prison didn't leave much room. I failed. Fixing that is top of my list after I leave."

"I don't see any flab."

Silence again. The balcony door was half closed, and the light streaming in gave the room a warm reddish hue. Again, he felt like he was in a film—and it suffocated him. He asked if she minded if he opened the door. She hesitated, then nodded. He got up, opened it, and light flooded in. She covered her eyes with a pillow. He looked outside at the buildings, rooftops, birds wrapping up their day. Zamalek was calm, but the world outside still hummed with a low, persistent buzz. He left the door ajar and returned to his chair. She was still. Slowly, she moved the pillow away from her face. Quiet.

She didn't seem in the mood to talk. He stayed silent too, sipping his coffee.

Then she began:

"His name's Chris. I met him here in 2010. He's a freelance reporter, wrote for American and British papers, news sites, any English-language outlet. He was kind, polite, smart, funny, thoughtful...a breath of fresh air after months of harassment by almost every male I met. A breath of reason and humanity—closer to what I was used to, how I was raised. Someone who understood my words, my gestures, my jokes, everything. It was bound to happen. We dated, then got married. All within three months."

"When did you split?"

"We didn't."

"Wait—you're married?"

"Yes."

"And where is he now?"

"In the States. He wanted to come with my mom and sister to meet me when I got out, but there wasn't enough time for them to fly over. The release date was postponed multiple times, then suddenly they let me out. I only found out hours before. And, honestly, it wasn't worth it."

"That's kind of sad."

"That he didn't come?"

"That you told your entire marriage story in under two minutes. How long did it last? Two years?"

"Yes."

"Two years in two minutes?"

"I could tell it in one."

"That's what's sad. Actually, it's depressing."

"You're being an ass."

"Didn't we agree on freedom of expression?"

"Go ahead. Express away."

"Anything I want?"

"You're literally my guest."

"Doesn't being here with me while you're married make you kind of a *sharmoota*?"

"Fuck you!"

"What? I thought we said freedom of speech?"

"Did I stop you from speaking? Fine, then hear this: I'm wondering if bringing you here was a huge mistake. Maybe you're just a lost, repressed, sex-starved boy. A rough, half-educated male who's going to dump his shit on me."

"That's fair."

"Now if you'll excuse me, I'd like to sleep a bit."

"Do you want me to leave?"

"I didn't say that. I said I wanted to sleep. Alone. If I wanted you gone, I'd say it. You can sit in the living room. Close the door behind you. There's music and books, food and drink in the kitchen, and a computer you can use, no password. Just don't tweet about me. At least not yet."

"I don't tweet. I don't post anything."

"Good. See you when I wake up."

***

Omar sat in the living room, not quite sure what to do with himself. After a while, he turned on the computer and started browsing. He never posted anything; all he did was read. He scrolled through his friends' posts. He followed many people online, but his own account was private.

He started with Facebook. Then Twitter. Then the news sites, one by one. The world, it seemed, was fine—everything following its usual course. Everyone was saying the same things they always said. Perfect. He tried to find Amal's profile but couldn't—too many 'Amal Mofeeds' and no photos. Maybe she had taken hers down because of the court case. Yesterday they'd reminded everyone not to post pictures of her from the party.

He shut the laptop and sat in the dark for a while. What was he doing here? Who was this woman, really? And why did he want to know her story? Why was he so harsh with her?

Something about her had gotten under his skin—no doubt. With her body, her ease, her naïve optimism, and everything else about her. She calmed him and unsettled him at the same time. Maybe he should have left early like Billy Crystal said, or at least at noon, after that first cigarette by the window.

He checked his watch: three-thirty. That was enough. He quietly gathered his things and walked toward the door. At that moment, the doorbell rang. Startled, Omar froze. He didn't even breathe. Didn't want the person at the door to hear him.

Silence. Then the bell rang again, longer this time. Still, he didn't move.

Then the person started knocking, insistently. Amal emerged from the bedroom in a white T-shirt. She gave him a questioning look; he shook his head, indicating he had no idea. She walked to the door and asked in Arabic:

"Yes?"

"Gas."

She rolled her eyes.

"One moment."

She went to her room, then returned wrapped in a long robe, opened the door and unleashed a brief but fiery lesson on manners and consideration. The man tried to explain, so she switched to English and gave him a longer lecture, venting all her anger while he stood there with his head down—Omar hidden inside the living room.

The man asked if she would pay the bill. She refused.

He asked if he could check the meter. She refused.

He lingered a bit, and she tilted her head with an expression that asked, what more do you want? He nodded several times and left. She slammed the door behind him.

Then she turned sharply to Omar.

"And where were you going?"

"I was leaving."

"Why? Don't we have an agreement?"

"Sort of."

"Sort of what?"

He paused, avoided answering.

"What? Cat got your tongue? Why were you sneaking out while I was asleep? So, you're immature and a coward? Speak! Express yourself! Or are you only good at insults?"

"What insults?"

"What you said about my marriage. What you said about me!"

"Didn't we agree to be honest?"

"I'm not blaming your honesty. You have the right to say what you think. I'm blaming what you think and say when you're being honest. What gives you the right to judge a person—two, actually—based on five or six sentences? Who do you think you are? Are you, like your president, a 'philosopher and doctor with divine inspiration'?"

"Why are you so sensitive? I told you what crossed my mind. If you don't like it, respond. What's with the censorship? If you can't handle a different idea or opinion, then what's the point of our agreement?"

Silence. From both.

"So why were you leaving?"

"I'm free to do what I want!"

Silence again.

"What's with the fucking darkness?" She demanded, "Are we still in prison? Turn on the light!"

He followed her gaze and saw the switch. He flipped it, and soft light filled the room. She went back into the bedroom. He sat down, a little angry, but not quite sure he wanted to leave. He spotted the cigarette pack, pulled one out, and lit it. He exhaled into the living room air.

Just as he was finishing the cigarette, she returned, now wearing a sleeveless orange dress, tight at the waist, flaring down to her knees. He looked at her and joked:

"What's this? *Too Young for Love?*"

She smiled.

"Look who's talking, Mister Twenty-One."

"Twenty-two."

She noticed the cigarette.

"Don't push your luck. Not in the living room!"

She opened the balcony door to air the place out and took the rest of the cigarette from his hand. Took a deep drag and blew smoke in his face. He reached for her waist, but she darted away.

"I think it's time to make some food. Come on, let's finish talking in the kitchen."

"I don't know how to cook."

"Liar. You told me the opposite yesterday at the party."

"So, you weren't completely drunk."

"My memory's coming back. Come on, I'll give you simple tasks. You can wash and chop vegetables."

He followed her, hesitantly, eyes fixed on the orange fabric wrapped tightly around her waist. He watched her hair cascading down her back, narrowing as it fell, like an arrow pointing at her waist. Her hips were hidden beneath the flaring dress, but the curve above them gave enough of a hint. He wanted to grab her, hold her close, crush her body into his until they fused into one—right here in the hallway leading to the kitchen. But he held back. He didn't want to be called sexually-starved again.

He kept his hands at his sides, but let his eyes roam, over her form, her movement, the little curve behind her knees, the tops of her heels, her hands, her neck beneath her hair, her shoulders, the tone of her arms, her brown skin. She sensed his gaze, turned slightly, with a hint of amusement. He met her eyes with the hard intensity she knew by now. She smirked and motioned for him to sit at the kitchen table.

She bent to grab vegetables from the fridge. He watched the lines of her body shift with the motion, her waist tightening, stretching, the fridge light casting a reddish glow on her knees, the muscles in her legs tensing. She handed him the vegetables; their fingers touched. They paused. Then, she gently withdrew. He looked into her eyes. She smiled, lips trembling slightly. He swallowed and laid the vegetables on the table. She handed him a large bowl. He took it, their hands lingering on it a moment too long.

She moved around the kitchen, back and forth, as the tension thickened, filled the air. He got up to wash the vegetables, standing next to her at the sink, not touching. She looked at him. He looked at her. Then he stepped away with his bowl, back to the table.

"Yalla! Tell me your story," she said.

"I don't want to. Not now."

"So, what? We'll just make food in silence?"

"No."

"So, what do you want?"

She stood in front of him, apron tied at the waist. He reached slowly for the knot. She didn't stop him. He tugged— she leaned forward. His hand moved along the dress, then unzipped it. It dropped between them. She stood still, looking at him. He pulled her gently toward him until his face touched her naked belly. She embraced him tighter. He wrapped his arms around her waist and pressed her to him. This was what he'd wanted exactly: her belly against his chest, her waist in his hands. He buried his face in her stomach. She leaned down, resting her head on his, tucking it between her breasts. He felt their softness and firmness on his forehead. He pressed in deeper. She pulled him tighter.

They crushed into each other.

He lifted his face—her lips met his eyes. Their mouths collided, breathless. She pulled back slightly to inhale. He smiled—for the first time—and sat her on his lap. They embraced again. He ran his hand through her hair, over her shoulders, chest, waist, legs, feet. He lifted her foot, kissed it. Then he knelt in front of her, and she took his place on the chair. He kissed her feet, her legs, her knees, her thighs, her pussy, her belly, her breasts. She stopped him, pulled his head back to her stomach, then to her pussy, running her fingers through his hair and pulling his head tighter. Then she slid down beside him on the floor, and they held each other quietly for a long time.

Then he fell asleep.

* * *

When Omar woke up, he found himself lying on a pillow on the kitchen floor. Amal was sitting on the other side of the kitchen by the window, looking at him, with a glass of white wine next to her.

"Slept well?"

"What time is it?"

"I don't know, probably five."

"Wow."

"See? You played the traditional man. You fell asleep and left me to make the food."

"I think the role of the traditional man is missing a scene before bedtime."

"Not at all, that's part of the role too. What? You think the traditional man fucks his woman every single day?"

He said nothing in answer.

"What? Did I shock you?"

"How about a truce?"

Amal fell silent for a moment, then walked over to him, sat beside him on the kitchen floor, leaned in, and kissed him.

"I'm sorry. You're right. That was unnecessarily rude."

"I didn't mean to upset you either."

Omar held himself back; he had almost apologized! That would've been a first. As he avoided the word 'sorry,' he realized he was using an earnest tone of voice he had only ever used sarcastically before. What was happening? And what was all that desire, that long embrace? It hadn't just been lust—he had longed for her closeness.

He looked at her and found her smiling pensively. She asked:

"Will you tell me your story now?"

"Sure."

"In detail."

As she spoke, she leaned in until her body was fully against his, her head resting on the pillow beside him, her cheek pressed to his right shoulder.

"Tell me."

"My story's a little strange. I was born in Paris."

"What? You?"

"What? Am I not the type?"

"No, you're not! Why were you born in Paris? Was your mother French?"

"No. Egyptian. But she was living with her husband in Paris."

"You mean your father?"

"No. She was married to someone else, then she met my father and got pregnant."

Amal laughed. "Okay, I am a *sharmoota* for sleeping with you—but it turns out you're an actual bastard!"

"I am. And she died giving birth to me. My father was studying in Paris and fell into depression after her death and left. He couldn't return to Egypt because he was wanted by the security services, so some Arabs in Paris helped him find a job in Sudan."

"And you?"

"He took me with him. We lived in Khartoum, but it turned out the investment company he was working for was actually a front for al-Qaeda. After some complicated drama, they were expelled from Sudan, and he ended up in Afghanistan. But he left me in Khartoum with the other children of the group, under the care of the wives who had stayed behind."

"What?! No, wait. Repeat that part."

"Which part?"

"All of it. What are you saying? Seriously? Al-Qaeda? *The* Al-Qaeda?"

"Yes, and I grew up in Khartoum with the rest of the group's kids."

"Al-Qaeda kids!"

"Yes."

"Until when?"

"Until my father came back from Afghanistan, just before 9/11."

"Hmm. And what was your father doing in Afghanistan exactly?"

"Fighting with the Arab *mujahideen*."

"Your father was a terrorist?!"

"Kind of."

"And you mock me because my father was an arms dealer?"

"I didn't mock. I asked."

"Wonderful. Great. And when did you come back to Egypt? And why?"

"I came back in 2009. My father came to Khartoum and took me."

"How did he get back into Egypt?"

"He sorted things out with the security services, somehow. I was still in Sudan at the time and didn't know exactly where he was. Then I had some serious trouble with the group—they nearly killed me—and he suddenly showed up and took me in 2009."

"They nearly killed you!? Oh my God! Really? I'm so sorry, I didn't realize your story was that dramatic."

"Appearances can be deceiving, Professor."

"Why did they nearly kill you? What did you do?"

"I joined another boy in trying to blow up the group's headquarters."

"What?!"

"We were fifteen at the time, me and the other boy. We hated them. We met an Egyptian intelligence officer in Khartoum who was looking for people to help him bring down the group, so we agreed. He gave us a bag full of explosives, and we carried it to the site of the group's leadership meeting. The operation nearly succeeded—we almost blew them all up. But Sudanese intelligence was monitoring the Egyptian guy and warned the group. So, they caught us, 'tried' us in a 'sharia court', and sentenced both of us to death."

"Are you sure you're not making this shit up? Please say you are!"

"I am not. The story is real and documented. Google it. Just type: 'Attempted bombing of the jihad group's headquarters in Sudan.'"

"Hold on."

She typed quickly on her phone, then began reading and mumbling:

"Oh my God! Seriously? Is this really you? Are you Musab or Ahmed?"

"Don't get hung up on the details. They're not precise."

"Oh my God! But they say the boy was actually executed."

"The other boy was. His father was on a 'jihad mission' outside Sudan and didn't know his son had been executed until he got back. But someone tipped off my father two days before my execution date, if I remember correctly, and he came and snatched me out of their hands. I didn't want to go. I preferred to die. Death felt like the proper end to it all. What really hurt was that the operation failed. I was ready to die if it had worked. I wanted to blow them all up."

"What the fuck! Truly! Your execution date? Blow them up? What the actual fuck? And then what happened?"

"Then we came back."

"And the Egyptian security services? They just let you be?"

"They took us in, of course. This was back in 2009."

"But the internet says this happened in 1995."

"Do you want to hear the story from me or from the internet?"

"Oh, I'm sorry! I'm just a bit puzzled. You know. I don't meet people who were nearly executed and tried to blow up other people before!"

"Well, now you have. And, by the way, you haven't finished your story."

"My story? After what you just said, I have no story my friend! Actually, come to think of it, it is a bit annoying that the Egyptian security service threw me in jail for receiving illegal funding, while you were roaming freely!"

"Do you have any fruit or something sweet?"

"Forget fruits! Are you armed?"

Omar laughed at the question. "No. I'm not into weapons."

"Right, you specialize in explosives."

"Don't worry."

"Don't worry?! Are you fucking kidding me? I'm seriously starting to consider running back to prison."

***

Omar sat on the bed, back against the wall, facing the window and its curtain drawn loosely across the frame. The room was small but high-ceilinged, like most of the old flats in Zamalek. Through the glass, he could see nothing but sky and the blank, weather-worn wall of the next building. From nearby apartments came the familiar Cairo sounds: raised voices, hammering, the persistent din of repairs. Beside him on the nightstand sat a large ceramic dish patterned in blue, white, and green with one chipped edge that interrupted the design. It looked like it came from Palestine. Or maybe Tunisia. Everyone in Zamalek seemed to have a dish like it, all slightly different, all chipped. As if they all came from the same source.

He didn't care for these apartments. Or this kind of furniture. They made him feel out of place. Even if he had the money, which he didn't, he still wouldn't choose to live here— or anywhere like it.

Across from him, Amal was eating a green apple she'd plucked from the dish. Slowly, deliberately, she chewed each bite in silence, watching him. Most of the apple was gone. She was working her way around the core now, grazing its edges.

"There must be a way to eat this part without ending up with all the seeds in your mouth."

"Yes, there's a way. It's called leave the damn thing— you've already eaten it all!"

"No, there are still these little parts left," she insisted.

"Do you really have to suck every drop out of it?!"

"Yes. Otherwise it's wasteful. And these parts make me sad. People always abandon them."

He sighed.

"Tell me—where did those muscles come from?"

"What muscles?"

She turned to him and patted his arm.

"These. And your abs. You look like an athlete, not some aimless taxi driver who sleeps all the time."

"Perk of being raised in the 'farm' of Northern Khartoum."

"Well, keep them."

"What are you thinking about?" He asked.

"I'm thinking that this early release will force me to face the accumulated cost of years spent putting things off—in the name of work, change, revolution, etc. I'm thinking my marriage died years ago, and I knew it, but kept pushing it out of sight so I wouldn't have to deal with it. I'm thinking Chris knows it too and pretends not to. I'm thinking that with all the freedom I supposedly have, I haven't been free, I haven't acted like a free person. I'm thinking our shackles are inside us. I'm asking myself what's the point of my work, what's the point of chasing freedom, what's the point of clashing with authority if the chains are inside us to begin with. I'm thinking maybe I wasted five years of my life for nothing, or almost nothing, in a miserable, broken country. And I'm thinking you're very young, and that I was drunk last night but I'm not drunk now, and I have no excuse for keeping you here. That's what I'm thinking."

"Do you want me to leave?"

"Stop asking that. I don't want to sleep alone tonight. That'll be my excuse: I'm anxious and miserable and I need company and affection, and you're the source of those things tonight. Or maybe my excuse will be that I just got out of prison, and I'm disoriented and angry. Or that I want to defy the rules and norms of this country that's fucked me with its rules and norms. I'll find an excuse. I'll write myself a justifiable one out of all this. But I want to hear the rest of your story, what happened to you after you came back from being a terrorist kid?"

"My story is long. I'm not sure I can string it all together. It's not just one story, it's many. Mine, my friends', my family's, people I met by chance. The past few years were unreal. I still can't believe all of it happened to me, or around me, in such a short time. I feel old. No joke. I feel like I've aged from everything I've been through."

"Why haven't you written those stories? Why not write them now?"

"I told you. I don't write."

"Shame."

"Although...I do know a writer who could."

"Who?"

"A novelist named Fishere. Limited talent, but he's a friend of my father's."

"Also a terrorist?"

"I don't think so."

"Why don't you take your stories to him?"

"He's busy these days."

"With what? Isn't he a writer?"

"He is 'safeguarding the democratic transition'."

"What?"

"Never mind. My stories aren't worth publishing."

"How would you know?"

"I just do."

"Why not ask this Fishere guy? Consult him—he's your dad's friend, isn't he?"

"Yeah, but he said and did some things that made me lose respect for him. I don't want to talk to him."

"OK, screw Fishere. Why not write these stories on your social media, then?"

"Like I said, I don't post anything. And I don't even like these stories. If I could, I'd erase them from my memory. The problem is they won't leave me alone, and I frankly don't know what to do with them. My father keeps telling me I need to get them off my chest. Unpack my baggage, so to speak."

"Why not tell them to me now and we can record them? Then put them online."

"Who would care to listen?"

"Why do you care if anyone listens? If the goal is to let them go, then here's your method."

"But they are all incomplete."

"I'll finish them for you, if you want."

"What do you mean?"

"Tell me what you have, and I'll fill in the rest, if it needs it. Hand me the phone. Let's try. Press that button. No, the one next to it. The red one, genius. Yes. Okay, let's begin with you and your terrorist father: tell me what happened after you came back in 2009. Let's see if you like the game.'"

2

Fakhreddine and Ayman
in the Desert

Friday, 6 p.m.

"We made it to Egypt in May 2009. As soon as we reached the edges of the valley—near Sohag—we sold the pack animals, bought regular clothes, ate, bathed, and cut our hair. We became normal people again."

"Wait—I'm confused. Which valley?"

"The Nile Valley. Oh, right, I forgot. We didn't come through the airport. Of course not. Neither Fakhreddine nor I had passports. And even if we did, we couldn't fly out of Khartoum airport. The Sudanese intelligence would've arrested us. It wasn't an easy journey. Fakhreddine took me through a route he knew across the Gilf Kebir desert, which he used a lot during his time with the group in Sudan."

"Very impressive," Amal said dryly.

"Anyway. We took the train from Sohag to Cairo. No more than two hours after arriving home, in Bein al-Sarayat, a plainclothes officer showed up and summoned us to the State Security offices. He asked us to come in the morning—which, according to my father, was both a generous gesture and a sign of confidence that we couldn't escape if we tried. We spent a wonderful evening with relatives I'd never met before: Maryam, the wife of my father's uncle—everyone calls her 'Aunt Maryam'—Layla, his cousin, and her son Tamer, who is about my age. I didn't say a word the entire time—not just because I didn't know them, but because I'd never had relatives. I didn't know how to act. It was the first time in my

44

life I sat with a family. On the 'Farm', we were raised as children of the group. We were raised to be disciplined and were kept at a distance from our actual parents.

"In the morning I went with my father to the State Security building. Everyone greeted him kindly, as though he worked there and had been away on vacation. After about an hour, we were taken in to see Major Ayman. He was poring over documents and didn't look up for several minutes. When he finally did, his stare was stern and scrutinizing. I later found out he was angry that Fakhreddine had left Bein al-Sarayat without his permission. That had been Ayman's main condition when he allowed him to return to Cairo and helped him settle in the neighborhood in 2001."

"Wait—your father had already come back to Egypt in 2001?"

"Yes, I told you—he came back after 9/11, in 2001. Focus!"

"But you didn't return until 2009?"

"Exactly."

"Why?"

"Why what?"

"Why did he leave you alone in Sudan for eight years?"

"Good question. Because he was taking revenge, as I told you."

"On whom?"

"On those who hurt him before. Can I continue the story?"

"Sorry!"

"Fakhreddine worked as a taxi driver during those eight years."

"Oh, so that's the taxi parked downstairs? That's your father's?"

"Exactly. He became a taxi driver even though he was a lawyer by training. The Security Services had already disbarred him in 2001. They allowed him to work as a driver on condition that he remain under the watchful eye of Major Ayman and his informants. When we returned in 2009, the whole country was on edge because the Minister of Interior had just been assassinated, shot dead in his own garden and among his bodyguards. The minister had come from State Security, so naturally the agency was on high alert and grasping at every possible thread.

"Ayman didn't know anything about Fakhreddine's jihadist past, or his time in Sudan or Afghanistan. All he knew was that Fakhreddine had disappeared from Bein al-Sarayat for nearly twenty years and reappeared in 2001 with an expired passport, claiming he had been in Libya and crossed into Egypt through the border. At the time, Ayman let him be, on the condition that he remained under surveillance, as I said. But Ayman wasn't a fool, he had a rather sharp instinct. He distrusted everyone and looked for signs and clues wherever he laid eyes. Fakhreddine's disappearances had become more frequent in recent months, each time with a different excuse. And now, suddenly, he reappeared with a fifteen-year-old son. Ayman felt this was just too much and decided to reopen his old file."

"Didn't you say the attempted bombing in Khartoum involved a collaboration with an Egyptian officer?"

"Yes, but that was an intelligence officer, not State Security. And it was a covert operation—only those directly involved knew the details. Ayman had nothing to do with it."

"Really?"

"Yes. But Ayman caught the scent with my appearance. He asked himself, *Who is this boy? Where has he been all these years? And why is he here now?* The logical questions. And with Fakhreddine dodging answers, Ayman grew more suspicious, like a dog after a bone. He swore he wouldn't let us go until he knew the full story. But my father insisted there was none. Naturally, Ayman didn't believe him. He questioned me but I didn't give him anything useful, either. He tried everything. He would let us go, then summon us again separately an hour later. Then release us, then call us back again—over and over.

"When asking about me led nowhere, he shifted to the past: what had Fakhreddine done between 1992 and 2001, where had he been, what were his activities during those years in Egypt, and what had he been up to during his repeated disappearances.

"The interrogation lasted for days. We didn't see daylight.

Most of the questioning focused on Fakhreddine, but, from time to time, Major Ayman would summon me, too. I only responded the way my father had coached me to during our journey back. I was young, but I was used to this type of intimidation. I wasn't afraid.

"Ayman began asking about my mother, and about my father's time in Paris before he supposedly moved to 'Libya,' and why he had left Paris. Then, he wanted details about Libya. Then, about how I was raised. We were held separately. No one mistreated us, but we saw no one and were not allowed to contact anyone.

"Ayman pored over Fakhreddine's file, scrutinized both of our statements, but found nothing that satisfied him. He wasn't a villain. He didn't necessarily hate Fakhreddine. He was just a regular State Security officer, obsessed with control, and was convinced that my father was making a fool of him. He was determined not to let that happen.

"The interrogation dragged on for weeks until Ayman got tired of us. Finally, he gave my father an ultimatum. He told him that he'd get the information one way or another—and that Fakhreddine would pay the price for stalling. He told us we would remain in detention until he got the answers he needed. Then, he would refer us both to court, and we would serve a very long sentence. That was Option One.

"On the other hand, if Fakhreddine cooperated, Ayman would let me go home and reduce the charges against him to a few years at most. At first, my father claimed he was fully cooperative and had no idea what Ayman wanted from him. Ayman named people who had indeed been with him in Paris and later in Afghanistan. Fakhreddine denied it all, but he began to feel the walls closing in. They kept circling each other for several more weeks until my father realized he had no real alternatives.

"So, he took option two. He admitted that he went from Paris to Khartoum, not to Libya as he had claimed, but denied any link to the jihadists in Sudan. He said he worked for an investment firm, and Ayman must be confusing him with someone else. Ayman pretended to accept this but asked further questions about Sudan.

"Ayman reminded my father that even crossing the border to Sudan in this way was a crime—not to mention that he had also used a fake passport at one point. He had fake Libyan entry and exit stamps on his real passport, and he had falsely claimed he had spent those years in Libya. That bundle of crimes—along with his recent illegal cross-border journey— was enough to land him in prison for years. My father admitted to all this, but nothing more.

"Deep down, Ayman knew the man in front of him was hiding more, but he had no solid evidence that would hold up in court. Torture wouldn't help—any confession made under duress would be inadmissible. Plus, Ayman was busy; he had more urgent cases than the mysterious travels of Fakhreddine. So, he treated these confessions as the cooperation he'd asked for. He offered my father a plea deal: confess to forging official documents, entering and leaving the country through unauthorized routes, and facilitating the activities of a group aiming to disrupt state institutions. In return, I'd be left out of everything. Fakhreddine accepted. He was referred to court and sentenced—on Thursday, January 20, 2011—to ten years in prison."

"Ten years? Really?"

"That's what happened."

"And you?"

"I was free to go. That was the deal."

"So, your father was in prison when the revolution broke out?"

"Yes."

"And he didn't get released with the others?"

"No. As luck would have it, his prison wasn't one that was stormed. So, he remained in prison the whole time."

"He was never released during everything that had happened?"

"No. He had dreamed of a revolution like that his whole life. and when it finally came, he was in prison."

"And you?"

"I found myself living with relatives I didn't know. But I

got to know them well—Aunt Maryam is eccentric, but wise and helpful. Aunt Layla is gentle and quiet. Back then, Tamer was cheerful and carefree, totally immersed in computers. I also met a woman named Dr. Shaimaa, who, from what I gathered from Tamer, had a thing with my father. There was mutual affection between them—perhaps more—but it wasn't entirely clear. She oversaw Aunt Maryam's treatment, became close to the family, and later co-founded a medical center in Bein al-Sarayat with Layla to help the elderly. Tamer helped them run it and managed their website. He wanted to launch a software company based on his web development work and had a major project I didn't understand at the time. I knew nothing about computers, but he taught me and said I was a fast learner. Eventually, he started the company, and I worked with him."

"And it succeeded?"

"Brilliantly. Mainly because Tamer knew practically everyone in Egypt with a computer. The company thrived, landed major contracts, and earned unbelievable sums—more than any of us had ever dreamed of. Tamer got married, and the family became financially stable for the first time. Fakhreddine was extremely proud of his 'kids,' as he called the two of us."

"How did you adjust to life in Cairo? How did you deal with girls? Did you go to university? And where did you learn English? Sorry, maybe I'm asking too many questions—it's just, I've never met anyone like you before. I've met ex-fighters, but never a young man raised in a terrorist camp!"

"I enrolled in a private school to get my high school diploma. After I graduated, I got into the Faculty of Commerce. My father suggested I study law, but I didn't want to. What good did law do for him or anyone? I picked commerce because it was easy. I slept through four years of college and graduated. I learned English online. I liked it. I liked music and wanted to understand the lyrics. And life is hard without English. Even at the 'Khartoum Farm,' we had an English teacher who taught us the basics."

"And girls? Life?"

"It's okay. Nothing dramatic. I'm not a very social person, but I have friends and acquaintances. Life went on."

"And your father? How was he in prison?"

"Back then, they allowed us to visit. I'd go every week. I was his main link to the outside world. I'd tell him what was happening in Egypt—my stories, my friends, the revolution, everything. He'd listen silently, but attentively. Occasionally, he'd comment on what was happening or on what my friends were doing. Personally, I played no role in the revolution. I didn't even participate at the protests."

"That's surprising! Why not?"

"Because I don't like big talk. I'd heard enough of it, and I'd seen firsthand how it leads nowhere. All those heroes, martyrs, all that talk of jihad—I'd had enough. I didn't want to deal with more of that. But my friends were in the revolution from day one, in different ways. They asked me to pass their ideas and plans to my father to get his opinion, but every time he'd say something different from what they wanted to hear. They started dismissing his views, saying he was part of the generation that failed. So, I tuned out news on the revolution. I'd just tell him what was happening in Bein al-Sarayat—about the family, the neighbors, the company, and of course, Dr. Shaimaa."

"And Shaimaa? Didn't she visit him?"

"No. She had no legal standing to do so."

"And the medical center?"

"Funny you ask. The center grew significantly after the revolution. Shaimaa and Layla got a grant to help them expand its services. A number of female doctors volunteered, and the center kept expanding until it was shut down in 2014 in what became known as the 'Bein al-Sarayat Case.' Everyone working there, including Layla and Shaimaa, was referred to the prosecutor. Tamer was furious and protested nonstop in front of the Interior Ministry. During one protest, he was arrested—charged with demonstrating without a permit—along with twenty others. He was sentenced to five years in prison. Dr. Shaimaa, Layla, and their colleagues weren't imprisoned, but their cases keep getting postponed every six months. The judge could decide to jail them at any hearing."

"Oh my God!"

"Right? And at the same time, the company's work declined until it stopped entirely—not just because Tamer was in prison, but because the economy itself came to a grinding halt. After a few months, we ran out of savings, and I had to find a new source of income. So, I went back to the old taxi."

"And that's how we met."

"And now we're caught up."

"Would you like more coffee? Or a beer, or a cigarette?"

"Could I have a piece of fruit?"

Amal reached for the patterned plate, picked up an apple and gave it to him. He took two bites, then put it back. Amal looked at the apple and waited for Omar to eat the rest of it. But he didn't.

"Aren't you going to finish it?"

"No."

"Okay, are you going to finish the story then?"

"Fakhreddine remained in prison until this summer. One day in June, his cell door opened, and they took him to the warden's office, where he found Major Ayman—now promoted to Colonel—along with an intelligence officer in civilian clothes.

"That wasn't the first time Ayman visited him. He had come in 2012 and told him he knew the whole story now—his ties to jihadists in Sudan and Afghanistan, the crimes he had committed in Egypt since returning. He told him the country was in the middle of a revolution, and the circumstances didn't allow for reopening the case. But he promised him that he wouldn't let him leave prison alive and advised him not to try or he'd be forced to take drastic action.

"This time, Ayman was back in the service and promoted! He was nicer to Fakhreddine, asked how he was, whether he was comfortable, and whether he wanted to get out. Fakhreddine, wary, asked him directly what he wanted. Ayman smiled—he didn't like beating around the bush either. He wanted help locating an old comrade of Fakhreddine's, a certain Sheikh Hamza, who was leading armed operations against the regime from the Western Desert, reportedly moving between Libyan, Sudanese, and Egyptian territories. Fakhreddine calmly refused. He said he wasn't a snitch and never would be.

"Colonel Ayman appealed to his patriotism, reminding him of the threat terrorism posed to himself and his family. Fakhreddine smiled and told him all his family was already in prison or awaiting prison sentences. The conversation turned into a sharp exchange, where each told the other what he really thought of him, rather bluntly. The meeting ended with Fakhreddine being sent back to his cell.

"But Colonel Ayman returned a few weeks later, as jihadist attacks intensified in Sinai and the Western Desert. He pressed again: 'For Egypt,' he said, 'For your children's future'— anything that might influence him. Traditional methods hadn't succeeded in catching any senior jihadist leaders in either Sinai or the desert. All they achieved was arresting foot soldiers, killing some during chases, and preventing occasional attacks. What they needed was someone who knew these leaders, their movements, their hideouts—someone who could navigate the vast desert as a terrorist, not as a policeman.

"Ayman entered into another long discussion with him. But Fakhreddine stood firm. He told Ayman clearly: the state he represents is a monster—both unbreakable and incurable—and Sheikh Hamza is similar. Fakhreddine wanted nothing to do with either monster. He had paid dearly in the past—lost his livelihood, hurt the ones he loved—and admitted defeat. He was out.

"That's when Ayman played his final card: the intelligence officer who had orchestrated the attempted bombing of the group's headquarters in Sudan through me. He brought him in without warning and told Fakhreddine who he was. My father was visibly shaken. The officer asked Ayman to leave them alone. Once they were alone, he told my father he had long dreamed of this meeting and never imagined it would actually happen. It only happened thanks to a mutual friend who connected him to Colonel Ayman.

"Fakhreddine asked dryly what he wanted. The officer said

he wanted to make amends for the harm he caused me—and to prevent further harm. My father understood what all this meant. They were using me now as leverage. Ayman finally got the full picture of both our pasts. And with my father already in prison, I was the only card left.

"The officer crafted a deal between Ayman and my father: my father would accompany Ayman's search party in the Western desert to capture Sheikh Hamza. In return, the Security Services would leave me alone, release Tamer and close the case against his family members, and, upon my father's return, he would receive a presidential pardon.

"They also took me to see him, and I begged him to accept. I told him that saving his family and himself was more important than all the grand ideals he might be sticking to. He listened quietly then said he would do it, for me. And so, he left with Colonel Ayman to track down Sheikh Hamza in the Western Desert."

"When was that?"

"Three weeks ago."

"And Tamer—was he really released?"

"He was."

"And the case against Laila and Shaimaa and all that?"

"Dismissed."

"And have you heard from your father since he left with Ayman?"

"No."

"Did he tell you when or how he would contact you?"

"He said he wouldn't contact me until the mission was complete and he was out of the desert."

"So, we don't know how this story ends."

"I can guess. I know the three of them well enough to predict what they'll do."

"What will they do?"

"My father and Colonel Ayman will spend weeks in the desert tracking Sheikh Hamza. In the end, my father will find him—because he knows all their hiding places. He trained many of them, so he will be able to predict their movements. He also knows how to find food and water in that desert thanks to his long journeys with the sheikh who founded the organization back in the 90s."

"Which sheikh?"

"You know, the one who founded Al-Qaeda."

"Seriously?"

"Yep."

"Carry on!"

"He'll find Hamza and his men, and there will be a shootout. Ayman will probably get wounded—he's not really a fighter. My father will capture Hamza—because he always does. Hamza fears him and feels guilty toward him.

"So, Fakhreddine will return leading a small caravan: the wounded Ayman and the captured Hamza. They will head toward a rendezvous point with the security forces, probably a spot accessible by helicopter and far from the scene of the confrontation.

"I can see it now: Hamza bound on one animal, Colonel Ayman wounded on another. But Hamza won't allow himself to be imprisoned by the Security Services. He knows what awaits him. He'll find a way to break free or grab a weapon.

"Of course, Colonel Ayman never parts with his official weapon. So he'll be the one armed when the standoff ensues. My father will be caught in the middle."

"Damn."

"You can imagine the situation. Ayman faces a terrible choice: if he shoots Hamza, Hamza will shoot my father, who is the only one that can take Ayman back to safety. Should he let a terrorist escape to save my father? He actually doesn't care about my father—an ex-terrorist. But he knows that my father is the one tending his wounds, guiding him in this desert to the pickup spot. He knows he won't survive on his own. If he shoots Hamza and Hamza shoots Fakhreddine, Ayman will likely die few days later.

"But if he lets Hamza go, what's to stop him from killing them both? There's no time to think or negotiate. I can see it—Ayman's finger is on the trigger, his gun pointed at Hamza, Hamza's gun pointed at my father. And in those few seconds, Ayman does what comes naturally to him: he fires. He hits

Hamza, who also shoots—hitting my father before collapsing. And so, all three fall in the desert—and die there."

After a pause, Amal exclaimed, "You're such a gloomy bastard!"

"Why? It's the logical outcome."

"Not at all. That's a contrived ending. There's nothing in the story that necessitates Hamza raising his weapon at Fakhreddine. Nothing forcing Ayman to act so stupidly, risking all three lives. You're projecting your own desperation onto the story!"

"Nothing forces people to act stupidly, but that's what they do. Don't you know the story of the scorpion and the turtle crossing the river?"

"I know it—but I also know many stories where not everyone dies. Let me tell you a more logical and better ending to your father's tale."

"Go ahead!"

"Most likely scenario: they go into the desert and fail to find Hamza. Finding terrorists isn't easy, especially in a desert that vast. Do you remember how long it took to find Bin Laden? And that was with the United States' might and all of their intelligence and surveillance technology. So, after a few weeks wandering the desert, Ayman and your father will return. He will be released. They'll go their separate ways.

"Second scenario: they find Hamza, arrest him, return without issues, and your father will be pardoned. Hamza is put on trial. Everyone moves on."

"You don't know these people."

"What people?"

"The jihadists, my father, or State Security."

"Even if they clash and someone is wounded, Ayman would never sacrifice your father. That would mean his own end too." Amal insisted.

"I told you—you don't know these people."

"And I told you—you're a gloomy bastard."

"Well, it's not like I turned out this way for no reason."

"Fine, tell me another story. One about your friends. I don't want to hear about terrorists and brutal security officers anymore. I'm sick of that whole generation. Tell me about someone your age."

"My friends? Easy. I'll tell you about Wael, Moheb, and Tamer. But can we eat first? It's dark out, and I'm starving. What time is it?"

"Nine o'clock. You're right. Let's eat."

3

Wael, Moheb, and Tamer
Meet the Unknown Party

Friday, Midnight

She studied his back—dark, unguarded. His skin was lighter there than on his face. His coarse black hair curled into small, stubborn spirals, scattered in no particular pattern. There were only a few stray hairs near the shoulders, then nothing—just smooth, bare skin down to the waist. *A woman's back*, she thought. Then, softly, she asked:

"Are you awake?"

"Yes."

"Will you tell me now?"

He nodded. She asked him to wait a second, pressed record on her phone, and placed it on the floor beside the bed. Now she was ready.

The room was dark. He lay on his side, his back to her. She considered asking him to turn around, then let the thought go. Better to just listen. His voice was beautiful. He considered turning toward her, then didn't. This way, he could speak as if to himself—no need to watch her face for signs of judgment.

Just a voice in the dark, unobserved.

He reached forward, drawing something invisible in the air.

"Picture three boxes on a computer monitor," he said. "The first one fills the screen. In the top right corner, a photo of a young man, wearing a baseball cap and smiling. You hear the click of a keyboard as the data begins to fill in:

Name: Moheb
Occupation: Software Engineer

57

Education: M.Sc. in Computer Science, Stanford University
Age: 26
Residence: Nasr City
Religion: Christian, Catholic
Hobbies: Football—Member of Al-Ahly Ultras

"Oh! I thought this was going to be a happy story."
"Now, a second box appears featuring a younger man, neither smiling nor frowning. He is brown-skinned with thin, sharp features and coarse hair:

Name: Wael
Occupation: Second-year student, Faculty of Commerce, Cairo University
Education: High school diploma
Age: 21
Residence: Imbaba
Religion: Muslim
Hobbies: Football—Member of Al-Ahly Ultras

"Finally, a third box: a young man with a kind, innocent smile. He has a thick nose and lips, and his small eyes are full of joy:

Name: Tamer
Occupation: Lawyer, software company owner
Education: Law degree, Cairo University
Age: 25
Residence: Bein El-Sarayat
Religion: Muslim
Hobbies: Football—Member of Al-Ahly Ultras"

"Is this Tamer, your cousin?"
"Yes. The three of them met in the stands at a match. Back then, the Ultras were just starting out. None of them were official members yet, but Moheb knew everything about Ultras groups worldwide. He followed them while studying in

Europe and later in the U.S.

"Football was his one passion. For four years, he lived and breathed the game—players, fans, teams. Moheb was obsessed with the European Ultras: their discipline, their teamwork, their self-reliance, their creativity. When he was in America, he traveled to Brazil, Argentina, and Chile, learning about the Latin version. He identified with the young men there who were just like Egyptians, scraping by, full of grit and brilliance, pulling off miracles on and off the field. He came back determined to do the same in Egypt. Through the contacts he'd made with Ultras from South America, he also made connections with groups in Europe. He returned to Cairo with the software degree his parents had dreamed of but was also nurturing the seed of his own dream.

"By the time he came back, others had already launched Ultras groups. He hovered around Al-Ahly and the stadium until he caught the thread and joined Ultras Ahlawy. With his knowledge of the global Ultras networks, he shot to the core of the group. Though he lived in Cairo, his eyes were on the world. Nothing happened in any Ultras group without him catching wind of it within days.

"In the stands, he stood shoulder to shoulder with hundreds of others, singing, chanting, moving as a single body, a single voice, a single will. They were a creature of many hearts, many minds, many arms and throats, solid as steel. In those magical hours, differences dissolved. Arguments, slights, bad blood—all of it melted under the roar of chants tearing through the air, filling these kids' ears and chests with confidence and strength. These were the best moments for him; nothing else felt as good.

"That's how Moheb—the globe-trotting son of Cairo— met Wael, the nearly invisible boy who had just been flung out of overcrowded Imbaba. Wael, who had to leave his home each morning just to breathe, to escape the single room and narrow kitchen where even standing was a luxury. He came from a house with no light, no sun. He fled to the Cairo University campus—the Commerce Faculty where he was enrolled."

"So Wael is your university colleague?"

"Yes, he was in my section. He practically lived on campus. There, he ate practically all of his meals, used the bathrooms, met friends, loitered. Sometimes, he even slept there. When the university was closed, he would wander over to cafés in Bein El-Sarayat and hang out with anyone who was around. On big match days, he always headed to the club's training grounds with the Ultras to hype up the team. If the match were less important, he would go straight to the stadium.

"Wael had never been part of a group before. He barely understood what the word 'group' meant. His family was large—six kids, a father, a mother, and a grandmother—piled together in their tiny house however circumstances allowed, each one fending for themselves however they could. The two girls fought for their freedom, for their right to education, pocket money, space, and new clothes like their brothers. The boys each defended what they saw as their own rights. The parents tried to keep the boat afloat and avoid clashes—sometimes by mediating, sometimes by intervening, and other times by ignoring, yelling, or pleading. They would do anything to get through the day, in the hope that tomorrow might bring something better.

"But this was not a group. Within it, he felt only a mixture of solitude and threat. That didn't mean there was no love, there was, but it was tangled with constant conflict. He never felt he belonged at school or—God forbid—university. The closest thing he had to belonging was his bond with the youth of Imbaba. He and they shared something unnamed: simply being from Imbaba. They recognized one another instantly in any crowd—'this kid is ours!' they would exclaim within seconds of seeing each other. That identity came with rights, duties, and unspoken boundaries, and it was the closest he had ever come to belonging.

"So, joining the Ultras opened a whole new world for him: he became part of a real group, a piece of a whole, with defined roles, rights, and responsibilities. His membership allowed him to do things he never dreamed of. It gave him power he never imagined he could have—and gave his life a meaning that surprised him. Without any fancy talk or clichés, he felt that his presence mattered, his absence was felt. He could come up with ideas and carry them out with the help of others. He could agree, disagree, contribute to something he couldn't achieve alone, and receive help with things he couldn't manage on his own. He gathered with others to do things they all loved. They laughed together—sometimes at their own failures, sometimes in joy over their achievements. They succeeded and failed, together.

"This was the only place where he mingled with youth from other neighborhoods and social backgrounds, and he didn't feel those differences created distance—quite the opposite. He found them useful. When he needed something, there were ten people ready to help, not just with football and cheering, but with studying, transportation, life advice, and of course, girls.

"Finally, we have Tamer, who met Wael through me, and both of them met Moheb in the Ultras. Tamer was always antisocial; he preferred being alone, in front of a computer. He was the king of the internet. Since 2009, he had been building websites and helping others build theirs. I think half of Egypt's bloggers launched their sites with his help, or at least half the bloggers I know. Back then, I was amazed that someone could earn money just by playing on a computer. I hadn't even touched one before or been online. Back in Sudan, our community considered the internet a 'source of evils.' Tamer was the one who introduced me to the digital world.

"Anyway, Tamer, spent most of his time in his room doing online things—some of which earned him money, most of which he gave to his mother. He would also sometimes take projects for free. His whole life was online—he even met his fiancée, Aya, online. The only exception was the Al-Ahly club and their games, which he followed religiously. It was natural for Tamer to join the Ultras. In addition to all the group's other activities, Tamer became responsible for managing their online presence.

"In the Ultras, the three became buddies. They went to the stadium together, stood and cheered together, traveled together to matches outside Cairo, usually in Moheb's little car. Tamer, who had money from his online stuff, often treated them to meals, and Wael usually got the tickets. Their friendship soon went beyond the stadiums. They met regularly at a café in Bein Al-Sarayat and helped one another whenever needed. Tamer helped Moheb a lot with his business, saving him thousands in software costs. Moheb's car served the other two in all kinds of situations, noble and not-so-noble. His tutoring helped Wael pass courses he couldn't have passed alone. Wael's loyalty and sincerity helped the other two more times than they could count."

"And then?" Amal prompted.

"Then the Revolution happened."

"Great. Here comes the gloom."

"Not yet. All three joined the protests on January 25. They saw the call on Facebook and decided to go to Tahrir Square. Over the next few days, they ran into most of their friends in the demonstrations. Tamer and Moheb went home at night to join their neighborhood watch, while Wael stayed in the square with those who camped there.

"Wael was happy, mainly because of the sudden freedom that had descended upon him. It was a wonderful feeling: sleeping in the street among strangers, with a general sense of safety drawn from sheer numbers, and for him, from having nothing to lose. Bassem, a journalist friend of Tamer, and his girlfriend Hend, took Wael under their wing, feeding him and keeping him company. That's where he met Mai, a classmate he'd glimpsed on campus a few times but never spoken to. Hend introduced them and told him Mai was a Revolutionary Socialist. He didn't understand what that meant but nodded approvingly. He asked Hend if she and Bassem were also Revolutionary Socialists. She said no—they were 'New Left.' He asked what the difference was. She started to explain but lost him two sentences later. Then, she introduced him to the rest of the crew with their various leftist and liberal labels. But they were all revolutionaries, and Wael just nodded. Tents appeared, food arrived, music and songs spread through the camp, and Wael decided he would stay in the square until

Mubarak left, or the army came and arrested them all.

"On the morning of January 30, Tamer brought his mother, Layla. Moheb came, too, with his entire family. For the next four days, this became routine: in the morning, Moheb and Tamer came with their families and supplies for those who had spent the night in the Square. They would stay until just past curfew, then return home. Were you in the square during those days?"

"Yes, since January 28."

"Right, the conspiracy!"

"You weren't there, were you?"

"No, but all my friends were."

"And what were you doing?"

"Sleeping most of the day, joining the neighborhood watch at night."

"Weren't you curious?"

"I was. I went with Tamer a few times, but I never stayed long. Anyway, enough about me. Anyone who was there says those days—from January 29 to February 2—were the golden days of the Square. Remember? It was a real celebration. A carnival of freedom. They said they realized how much they had been repressing themselves, voluntarily, in anticipation of the state's punishment. Suddenly, all that repression was lifted, and from each of them came thoughts, dreams, and actions they didn't know they had. They felt they had grown—not in age, but in size, in the space they occupied. It was as if the air, the streets, and the people belonged to them too, or were part of them, or part of the space they now roamed freely. Before, invisible threats had hemmed them in and driven them inward. Now, they were expanding."

"Yep, of course I remember that!"

"And, of course, with freedom, came love. Wael's relationships with women before had been sparse and messy; his experience was no more than stolen kisses followed by fights or a slap in the face, or paid encounters. Suddenly, he found himself face to face with a real girl looking at him with real affection. He felt something stir inside him that he never knew existed. Like in movies, they both realized they were 'falling in love,' and laughed at the shared discovery. It didn't even need saying; they simply were. He reached out and held her hand. He didn't need to muster courage or seek advice from Moheb or Tamer. He didn't panic. He just did what felt most natural. He held her hand with a smile, and she rested her head on his shoulder. What happened between Wael and the revolutionary socialist that night wasn't sex—it was a deep, mutual, warm, blissful connection. When the call to dawn prayer rang out from Omar Makram Mosque, Wael felt that he could do anything. That the world was open. That his life was his own, in his own hands."

"And what about Tamer and Moheb?"

"Moheb wasn't in a relationship. His focus was on his family, work, and the Ultras. His mother was the most important person in his life, and his sister. He felt responsible for them, especially since his father had passed. When he brought his family to the square, he made sure to protect them from anything that might put them off, like the niqabis, Salafis, or Muslim Brothers. You remember those were the days of Christians protecting Muslims during prayer and the niqabi woman hugging Christian girls—all that nonsense. But, of course, there were other stories, too. Not everything was perfect and peaceful coexistence. Moheb tried to keep his family away from those other things; he didn't want to lose their support for the protest.

"Tamer, on the other hand, found himself surrounded by dozens of his friends, especially bloggers he'd helped over the years. When the internet came back, he got busy helping them to organize and improve their online coordination. His fiancée, Aya, grew closer to his family and bonded deeply with his mother, Layla. Shaimaa, the doctor and Layla's business partner (and my father's 'friend'), was also there—but she and Layla spent most of their time at the field hospital."

"And then what? When are we getting to the terrible part?"

"Well, the real story began on February 2, with the arrival of the camels in Tahrir Square. But I have to tell you the story of three other people first before we talk about camels."

"More people! I am getting lost!"

"You asked for stories, I am giving you stories."

"Fair enough. So, I need to shelve Wael from Imbaba, Tamer your cousin, and... who is the third?"

"Seriously? Moheb!"

"Right. Moheb the good Christian."

"Good. We will just take a short break from them. Now, imagine three new frames on the screen. In the first, you see a man in his mid-forties, with a reserved smile:

"Name: Saeed
Occupation: Marketing manager at MSA Insurance
Education: B.A. in Humanities
Age: 46
Residence: Mohandessin
Religion: Muslim
Marital Status: Married, father of three
Hobbies: Watching TV, hanging out with friends, smoking shisha

"In the second frame, you see a thin, dark-skinned man. He is a bit younger than Saeed, with unkempt hair, and eyes that seem restless:

"Name: Habashy
Occupation: Employee at the Ministry of Transport
Education: B.Sc. in Agriculture
Age: 35
Residence: Haram
Religion: Muslim
Marital Status: Married
Hobbies: Reading and travel

"Then, the third frame appears, with a dark-skinned young woman flashing a broad, radiant smile. She's slender, with long, straight black hair. Her eyes also smile, gleaming with warmth:

"Name: Rasha
Occupation: Teacher
Education: B.A. in Education, English Department
Age: 28
Residence: Haram
Religion: Muslim
Marital Status: Single
Hobbies: Embroidery, glass painting, music, and dancing

"Now, imagine it is February 2, in Tahrir Square, just before the Camel Battle. We see these three walking through the Square, chatting with strangers.

"Saeed is talking about the state of the country, and all the things he sees going wrong: traffic, taxes, education, healthcare—and what things should look like. He worries about his children's future, given the direction the country is taking.

"Habashy is complaining about the government's dysfunction. He says that he has worked at the Ministry of Transport for ten years, and his salary, after 'bonuses' and 'incentives,' barely reached 800 pounds a month. His wife also works, but she only earns around 600. How are they supposed to live on that? Should they take bribes? Embezzle ministry supplies? Work a second job? And when would they live if they did? What if they want children? What future awaits them in this career? Should they quit the civil service? But what else can they do, with no experience beyond government work?

"Meanwhile, Rasha is listening to these conversations, looking both bewildered and exhilarated. She shares their problems—and more. She wants to talk about what it's like to be a girl in a society that sees her as prey—or, at best, a 'fruit'. She wants to talk about the constant fear: fear of being groped, fear of being humiliated, of the police, of their presence as of their absence, of a knock on the door or an unknown phone number, of taxi drivers, of bus passengers, drivers, vendors, pedestrians. She wants to say that, for the first time, she feels safe—here, among thousands of strangers who smile at her, make way for her, help and protect her. She wants to say all that, but she's more eager to keep listening. And just then, the camels appear, bursting into the square.

"Of my three friends, Wael was the only one in the square that day. When he saw the camel riders charging, he immediately called Tamer, Moheb, and others from the Ultras to come rescue him. Within the hour, they all arrived, pouring into the square without thinking about the politics of it. They came as soon as they heard, and without hesitation, joined the protesters in their battle against the camel riders.

"It was a shitshow. The clashes had no defined front lines, and the violence was everywhere. It took hours for the square's defenders to push the riders back to the periphery. But at the beginning, Saeed, Habashy, and Rasha nearly lost their lives—and certainly would have if not for Wael, Moheb, and Tamer.

"Wael pulled Rasha from beneath the hooves of a charging camel and the swinging sword of its rider. Just like in the movies, he grabbed her as the camel's hooves hovered in the air above her, and she screamed beneath them, staring at death. God knows what ran through her mind in that moment, but Wael saw her, and in an instant, he yanked her by the arm and hurled her to the side. The hooves struck the ground, and the sword slashed through the air. Who knows where it landed, perhaps on someone else. The rider, enraged, chased Wael in a fury.

"Wael ran like he'd never run before, leaping onto a metro ventilation station. The camel hesitated for a moment—just long enough for Wael to gain ground. He ran until he disappeared down Mohamed Mahmoud Street. He never saw Rasha again—she, too, had left the square. But he was satisfied with what he had done."

"And what about her? Where did she go?"

"She went home and didn't return to the square for a week. Habashy's case was different. Tamer and his friends found him lying on the ground, being beaten by four thugs. One of them kicked him in the stomach. Another gripped a heavy club and kept bashing his head, over and over. Habashy, a thin man, quickly lost consciousness under the blows. His head was drenched in blood, but that didn't stop the man with the club from continuing, methodically. Tamer and two others shouted at the attackers, trying to guilt them into stopping. The men turned and cursed them and then continued the beating. There was no choice but to engage them. Tamer reached out and dragged Habashy away slowly while the other two distracted the attackers until four more Ultras arrived and scared the thugs away. Tamer carried Habashy on his shoulder to the field hospital near Mohamed Mahmoud Street. The doctor— or someone who claimed to be one—shook his head grimly as he worked to stop the bleeding, clean the wound, and dress Habashy's head all at once. Tamer asked: 'Will he live?' The doctor gave a noncommittal answer, but he did live. He regained consciousness that evening. Tamer helped transfer him to a hospital where a fellow Ultra was a doctor. Gradually, Habashy's condition improved. He survived and told Tamer he owed him his life. The bruises remained visible on his head for a while, and the injuries gave him bouts of headaches, but he lived.

"As for Saeed, the insurance marketing manager, he ran into another gang of thugs. Their leader brandished a sword in his face and swore to slice him in half. Moheb disarmed him—no one knows how. Moheb wasn't a fighter, certainly not built for combat. He was a mild-mannered, respectable guy who probably hadn't been in a fight since middle school. But some kind of courage seized him when he saw the thug raise the sword overhead with both arms. Moheb came from behind, saw the blade and the terrified look on Saeed's face, and grabbed the man's wrists, yanking them down with strength that seemed to come from nowhere. The thug hadn't seen him coming. He lost his balance and fell sideways. That was enough for Moheb and his friends to tackle him, tie his hands and legs, and restrain him. A few other guys joined and tried to drag him through the square to lynch him, but Moheb and his friends refused. They carried the man—whose comrades had fled—to the Square's edge and handed him over to a military police officer. Saeed was in shock for a long time.

He had seen death—felt its certainty in the moment he stood alone before the swordsman. There had been no escape for him. No way out. None of his pleas or threats had swayed the man. Then, suddenly, a stranger saved him. A week later, once he'd recovered from the shock, he searched for Moheb to thank him. But he couldn't find him. He didn't know his name, but he remembered his face clearly. He returned to the square with his wife and three children several times to look for him. He wouldn't find him until a year later. And even then, he wouldn't be able to thank him.

"The year following the Camel Battle would change everything for all three of them."

"Which three?"

"Moheb, Wael, and Tamer."

"What about the other three?"

"Would you just let me tell the story, or would you like to take over?"

"Calm down, Scheherazade! Tell it your way."

"After that day, Moheb threw himself fully into the revolution. It wasn't a conscious decision, he just slipped into it, little by little. Its events filled most of his day, and, though he kept telling himself he'd return to work tomorrow, 'tomorrow' always came with deeper involvement in revolutionary stuff. With time, going back to work began to feel like going back to the gym after a long break: something you know is good for you, even necessary, but that you keep postponing. The economic slowdown helped excuse his absence. Were it not for his sense of duty toward his mother and sister, he might have abandoned work altogether.

"His mother had worked hard to cover the costs of his education without compromising the family's social standing or standard of living. Moheb understood this well. Since returning, he'd been committed to repaying her for the strain and anxiety she had endured to strike that difficult balance. She'd taken out loans using a piece of land she owned as collateral, and Moheb had paid them off. He'd also set aside money for his sister's eventual wedding. From time to time, he would surprise them with a trip, fancy clothes, or a piece of jewelry, which made him very happy—probably more than they themselves were.

"So, he couldn't walk away from the company he had built and devote all his energy to the revolution as he wished to do. He kept showing up, answering client queries, closing a few deals, updating some software products for sale, but only enough to keep the company going. This was no longer his primary occupation. His real focus was the revolution.

"He attended protests every Friday, and every other protest, too: protests against harassment, against some decision by the Military Council that took charge when Mubarak stepped down, or against the absence of a law that was needed, against this and in favor of that—people took to the streets so many times and for so many causes during that first revolutionary year that it is hard to keep track. Moheb also joined every Ultras protest. When he wasn't demonstrating, he was helping fellow activists build new initiatives or coordinate between existing ones, whether online or at party offices, cafés, or the homes of prominent political figures.

"His mother and sister were much less enthusiastic. 'The Islamists are lurking and will seize control,' they warned, 'the population is mostly illiterate and can't choose for itself,' 'these divisions will destroy the country.' Moheb shared some of these doubts, but he pushed them aside. He kept trying to reassure his mother and sister—as if to reassure himself. He'd say: 'We've started down this path. There's no turning back. It's too late.'

"Then came the presidential elections. Moheb's friends split across three campaigns: for the former Muslim Brother-turned Democrat Aboul Fotouh, for the Nasserite Hamdeen, and for the liberal Baradei. There was something appealing about joining Aboul Fotouh's campaign, particularly since Moheb was Christian—it would show some solidarity above religious boundaries. Many of his friends pressured him to do so. But in the end, he felt more at ease with Baradei's team. Moheb didn't have a fixed political identity—he wasn't a Socialist, or a Nasserist, or, of course, an Islamist. That's why Baradei's campaign felt like the right fit. All he wanted was to live in a functioning country, like the ones he'd seen in Europe and America. A country with proper roads and organized traffic, public services, an elected government, and opportunities for people to learn, grow, and move forward in life without arbitrary obstacles. He wanted to live in a country that made sense, not one that defied logic at every turn.

"Moheb used to tell his friends that what drives him mad about life in Egypt is its constant defiance of reason. A car driving against traffic makes no sense, but worse, the driver often finds it necessary to do so because the traffic flow itself is illogical. If he followed the rules, he'd never reach his destination. 'We shouldn't have to live like this,' Moheb would repeat to himself and to others. That's what pulled him into the revolution: a hunger to straighten what had gone crooked, to restore some functionality. You want to start a business? It shouldn't be torturous. Want to buy or sell something? These are the steps. Want treatment, or to learn or teach something? Here's how. The state should facilitate and regulate—not obstruct and censor. It should help people, not complicate their lives or interfere with their choices.

"That was all he wanted, to live like an ordinary citizen lives in the UK or Chile or Argentina, or any of the lucky places blessed with decent governments. For him, the revolution was a scream of how fed-up everyone was. It wasn't about ideology, and it wasn't for high-flown speeches. That's why he picked Baradei over Aboul Fotouh's Islamist-tinged campaign or Hamdeen's nostalgic Nasserism, neither of which he stomached.

"He had no formal role in Baradei's campaign. Sometimes he helped build and manage its online platform. Other times, he found himself in meetings discussing strategy or the electoral program, or prepping Baradei's media appearances. It all happened by chance. He'd be sitting with someone, and another colleague would show up and ask him about something, then take him along to a meeting. Or he'd strike up a conversation with a campaign leader who liked his ideas and asked him to write them up, or to attend a meeting to present them. That's how he met Baradei, several times. Once, they ended up alone for nearly an hour. Moheb told him everything he felt—from admiration to his hopes that Baradei would take responsibility—touching on a hundred ideas he saw as important. Baradei nodded, replied now and then, but often changed the subject and asked about people Moheb didn't know.

"Other than his work on the campaign, Moheb was present in every confrontation that took place between protestors and the authorities that year, including the brutal Mohamed Mahmoud Street events, where he lost a friend to the security forces. And despite all of this, he didn't miss a single Ahly game. In fact, he became more active with the Ultras, who succeeded in everything they planned despite interference from the authorities. Moheb took pride in their success and would say to his friends: 'This is what we can achieve even with the state screwing us over—imagine what we'd do if they left us alone! Or helped us! Now imagine if we applied this model to the economy, education, healthcare, the arts, administration!' That was his revolutionary dream: for the state to help people like him—or at the very least, get out of their way.

"Now, let me move on to Wael. He spent that year roaming the streets with Mai, the Revolutionary Socialist. They joined every protest and event, especially those involving confrontations with the security forces, always on the front lines. But on the first day of the Mohamed Mahmoud clashes, Wael voiced his objection. He thought these clashes were pointless and refused to join. He was standing with Mai at the corner of Mohamed Mahmoud Street and Tahrir Square while protestors were rushing in all directions. Reports of the wounded kept pouring in. When Mai urged joining in, he asked her: who's fighting whom? And for what? 'For whose benefit are we supposed to walk into a street where bullets are flying from the Interior Ministry?' he asked. Mai grew furious. Her sensibilities as a Revolutionary Socialist were hurt and she accused him of thinking only of his own skin. 'When unarmed citizens face a fully armed security force,' she said bitterly, 'it's not a moment for analysis. It's a moment for action, clear and simple. But it seems that your primary allegiance is to yourself and yourself alone!' Then she turned and ran into the street leading to the Ministry of Interior.

"Wael lit a cigarette, took two drags, shrugged, and walked off to his usual café near Tahrir. He sat there sipping tea, then coffee, then a cinnamon drink. But when the motorbikes began arriving with the wounded, and news of dead protestors spread, he leapt up in a panic and ran to find her.

"Slowly, he made his way toward the frontline. The place looked like Ramallah during the Intifada as he'd seen it on TV: an empty street, abandoned buildings, bricks and debris strewn across the pavement, a young man crouching behind a car and popping out now and then to hurl something across. The air reeked of smoke and gunpowder. Tear gas canisters exploded every few minutes. Sometimes a protestor, face-masked, would grab one before it blew and throw it back. Two young men were pushing a large dumpster, shielding themselves behind it. Then came gunfire. One hurled a Molotov cocktail. Then more fire. And more smoke.

"He saw a familiar face and asked him if he'd seen Mai. The man pointed vaguely forward: 'She's up there.' Wael walked forward, cautiously, until he could see the shooters from the other side. Still, no trace of her.

"Then, behind one of the last dumpsters before the no man's land that separated protestors and the Interior Ministry building, he saw a Molotov-thrower that could be a woman. Mai had debated with him many times over the difference between state and revolutionary violence. She asked why revolutions had to remain peaceful when the state used every form of force to crush them. 'Revolutionary violence,' she said, 'was necessary to dismantle tyranny and build a new order.' He'd responded with the usual commonsense arguments—that the state had legitimacy from its role and public consent, while the revolution was representing a minority. She dismissed that outright, scoffing: 'What consent? The kind extracted through fear and repression. When did this consent happen? And what about the people's support for the revolution—doesn't that give it a comparable right?' Wael wasn't great at arguing. He admitted as much. He wasn't a revolutionary thinker like her. She'd mock him when he said that: 'Anyone is a revolutionary thinker, once they shed the nonsense they've absorbed from media, school, and other apparatuses of ideological control.' Their debates were endless, but largely harmless; it boiled down to marching in a protest, reposting something online, or spraying a slogan or two on some street wall. But now there were guns, and people were getting shot.

"Was it really her, throwing that gas canister at the shooters? No, it wasn't her. He kept looking, searching those deserted buildings. After half an hour, it became clear she wasn't in the area, so he gradually pulled back the same way he came and returned to the café—only to find her sitting there, rubbing her hands nervously while talking on the phone. When she saw him, she dropped the phone, stood up, and ran straight into his arms. He held her tightly while she sobbed and apologized, and he apologized too, pulling her closer. Then he said something that made her laugh through her tears. She playfully smacked his chest when he joked that he'd gone into the clashes to join the revolutionary violence but didn't find her there.

"They drank a lemonade, then returned to the square and helped carry the wounded. Later, they went into Mohamed Mahmoud Street together and each hurled a Molotov cocktail toward the security forces. Wael took lots of pictures of the fighting, and about an hour later they returned to the Square.

"But those were the dramatic peaks of the revolution. Most other days were peaceful marches and sit-ins, and lots of coordination meetings. These took place in downtown offices, campaign spaces, friends' apartments, cafés, restaurants, or often just on the sidewalk. None of these meetings or initiatives led to any tangible achievements, which frustrated Wael—but Mai seemed content.

"One day, he asked if she planned to join any presidential campaign. She emphatically said no, mocking Baradei, Aboul Fotouh, and Hamdeen in turn—calling the first an unreliable dreamer, the second unsure if he was rightwing or left, and the third confused between history and ideology. None of them, she said, would bring about anything useful. He asked her what was useful. 'This,' she said. 'What we're doing. These revolutionary efforts.' When he pointed out that they had failed to achieve a single goal, she shook her head in gentle reproach, assuring him that everything was going according to plan. 'Change doesn't come overnight. The people won't find bread, freedom, and social justice without a struggle, without *learning* to struggle.' That, she said, was the purpose of this phase: building a movement, raising awareness, shaking entrenched norms. That's what lays the groundwork for future change.

"Wael wasn't convinced, but he went along. Through these meetings, Wael met many people, but he only had eyes for Mai. When one or two women tried to flirt with him or suggested he should 'open up' his relationship with Mai, he rebuffed them. Mai would sometimes test him, even encouraging him to flirt with others. That unsettled him more than anything else. Once, for his birthday, she arranged for a friend to join them in bed, explaining the experience as a form of freedom—a way to separate their choice to be together from pressure or social conditioning. He freaked out.

"Alongside protests, clashes, discussions and coordination efforts, Wael spent the year cheering for Al-Ahly with his Ultras friends. (He also passed his college exams—something he credited more to the administration's leniency than to any real progress in his learning) He went to every game, sometimes taking Mai along. Mai wasn't an Ahly fan, not even into football, though she hid that from Wael). Still, she never got in the way of his Ultras involvement. On the contrary, she encouraged it. She saw the Ultras as a powerful force with revolutionary potential. If they became what they should be— given their working-class majority—they could become a first-rate revolutionary force. She knew Wael hated theory and didn't expect him to raise the group's class consciousness, but she encouraged him to stay involved. At least it was a foothold. And someone else, she was sure, would push the ideas forward.

"But the idea of 'opening the relationship' kept coming back. She argued that an open relationship was healthier, that it allowed love to last. Everyone, she argued, is attracted to other people. Instead of bottling up those passing attractions and letting them poison the relationship, opening it allowed them to be addressed for what they were—fleeting attractions. A night here or there didn't threaten her place in his heart or his in hers. 'It's just sex,' she declared.

"At first, he thought she was pulling his leg. Then, he wondered if she was interested in someone else or trying to end their relationship. In the end, he said that even if her logic made sense, he didn't want it. He told her he loved her—her, specifically. That he was happy with her, comfortable with her, in bed and out of it. He didn't want to seek out others. But she wasn't convinced. Finally, he told her to choose either him or those unknown other people. She chose him but made clear her objection to the monogamous model.

"Toward the end of the year, he invited her over for lunch at his family's place. She agreed, met his mother and whichever siblings happened to be there. His mother wasn't used to girls like Mai, but she kept an open mind, saying the world was changing and it was better to see things for herself than be left in the dark. She actually liked her—she was educated, from a good family, clearly attached to her son, and nice to everyone. Still, she couldn't fathom Mai's messy hair! She asked her if it was naturally like that or if she'd done something to make it look messy. On the way home, Wael and Mai argued, not about his mother's comment, but about poverty. Mai said she loved Imbaba, everything there felt real and genuine: its narrow alleys, its kind, worn-down people, its poverty. Wael snapped, called her pretentious, said she didn't know what she was talking about, that she was faking sympathy. Mai was stunned. She asked the microbus driver to stop and got out in the middle of the street. Wael stayed. He didn't look back as the microbus pulled away. She didn't look at him either.

"As for my cousin Tamer, his work took off. Half of it was volunteer work but the other half brought in more money than he'd ever seen. He connected with programmers and developers, opening doors and bringing in more projects and revenue. His success made everyone happy: his mother Layla, Aunt Maryam, even his imprisoned Uncle Fakhreddine—and, of course, Tamer himself. With this financial success, he could finally marry Aya, his longtime fiancée. Aya suggested they buy an apartment in a nice neighborhood, but Tamer refused to leave Bein al-Sarayat where he grew up. They found an apartment close to his mother's. And so, they moved in together, greeted by ululations and congratulations from the entire neighborhood.

"Tamer began to discover what life looked like with money—its freedoms, and distractions. He had employees now, paid them salaries, and needed to manage them: supervise, guide, scold, sometimes fire. He had more money than he needed, so he started thinking about investments. He gave a lot to his mother, and to the medical center she ran with Dr. Shaimaa.

"The one thing he couldn't do, with or without money, was get Fakhreddine released, whether on medical grounds, a pardon, or anything else. He tried everything: revolutionary friends pressing their new contacts in the state, personal connections from work, even media campaigns to spotlight the case. Nothing worked. What the money did do was improve his uncle's prison conditions and the care he received behind bars.

"Like with Moheb and Wael, his new circumstances did not stop Tamer from cheering for Al-Ahly with the Ultras. He did go less regularly, though. But he made up for his absences by smoothing over tensions between the club administration and the security services. He, Moheb, and Wael often laughed about the irony: the boy from Bein al-Sarayat who used to borrow money to buy a ticket was now the well-off guy smoothing obstacles and calling in favors from high places. There was a revolution indeed!"

"I'm bored," Amal interrupted.

"You're the worst listener in the history of storytelling. Do you want me to stop?"

"No, I just want a break. I'll go to the bathroom, then get

a drink and come back. Why don't you have a cigarette?"

"Look at you—encouraging me to smoke?"

"Stop whining. Do what you want. I'll be right back."

Amal got out of bed and walked to the bathroom. It was close to 3 a.m. Omar felt tired but didn't want to sleep. He got up, too, went to the kitchen, and made himself a cup of tea. From the bathroom, she heard the boiler and called out laughing,

"Are you seriously making tea?"

He asked if she wanted some.

She laughed, "I'll make myself a real drink."

He returned to the window, sat on the ledge, and lit a cigarette. She joined him with a glass of something colorful. He looked at her.

"Go on. Finish that tedious story."

"If you're tired, I can stop."

"If I wanted to sleep, I wouldn't ask your permission. I just needed a drink. I know where this story is going, and I need something to brace myself for it. So, bring it on."

"Fine. The three of them—Moheb, Wael, and Tamer—went to that game in Port Said."

"I knew it! Damn you!"

"The day began like any other game day. They met at the buses, but then a message from the organizers told them the bookings had been canceled by the bus company, fearing violence. Everyone would have to take the train instead. They bought water bottles, snacks, and headed to the train station where they boarded with the rest of the Ultras. Some were nervous about what Al-Masry supporters might be planning. Others were more worried about possible police traps, especially after all the Ultras anti-police and anti-military chants in recent games. But my friends weren't unusually concerned. It would be a tough game against a strong team that had notoriously tough fans- but that was the Ultras' job: to support their team when the game was hard.

"The Ultras leaders walked through the train cars, reminding everyone to avoid confrontations and keep things calm. Apart from that tension, the trip was like any other—

some sang, others slept. At Ismailia, one stop before destination, the Ismaily fans threw stones at the train, as they usually do. Once they arrived at the stadium in Port-Said, however, they became really anxious. As you know, the match events took a dark turn. Al-Masry fans kept storming the field. Everyone thought the game would be canceled, but it wasn't. By halftime, the unease had spread. My three friends searched their comrades' eyes for the usual reassurance but found none.

"Everyone was anxious. Cheering—louder and more defiant—became their collective shield. As if, by raising their voices, they could push the danger away. But fear was creeping beneath the noise. It felt like when you hear noises in a dark apartment and you're alone. You speak loudly, move with confidence, trying to scare the fear away. But then the sounds get louder, and the suspicion solidifies: something's actually there. It is not a ghost, it is not your cat, it's an intruder, aiming a weapon at you. And you are unarmed, powerless.

"Their fear increased when some Masry fans broke onto the field at the end of the game, chasing the Ahly players, while the police did nothing. Then Al-Masry fans swamped the Ahly Ultras section. The security forces who had been standing between the two sections quietly withdrew, leaving a clear path open. The front rows of the Ultras tried to hold the line but pulled back as they saw blades in the attackers' hands.

"Suddenly, they realized that this was an ambush, and the anxiety turned into panic, with everyone scrambling to escape. They ran toward the rear exit but at that moment the lights went out. Only the red glow of flares lit the stands, casting eerie shadows. Screams filled the air. When they reached the doors, they found them locked. The trap was complete.

"The attackers didn't look like normal fans—they were something out of a horror movie. Blind stabbing at faces and stomachs. Shrieks. This wasn't a brawl you could break up or de-escalate. It was pure, unleashed madness, bringing death to whoever was in its path. Moheb rushed toward the locked gate, then turned and ran up the stands, trying to flee from that corridor of death. But one attacker spotted him and pointed him out. Two others followed. Moheb looked around, searching for an exit, a hiding place, someone to intervene. He looked at their faces, but there were no human faces there, no expression, no connection. Pleas, threats, silence—nothing reached those dead faces. The three advanced. Moheb stood frozen. Helpless. They grabbed him as he struggled and threw him over the edge of the stands. He hit the asphalt headfirst and died instantly.

"Wael and Tamer were together when five men attacked them—armed with blades and other weapons Tamer couldn't make out in the dark. One of them kicked Tamer in the stomach, knocking him down. As he struggled to rise, he saw the other four surrounding Wael, beating him mercilessly. The kicks came fast and hard. Wael writhed in pain, unable even to shield his body.

"Tamer froze. In the pitch-black moment, their eyes met— Wael's gaze reaching for him like a lifeline. But Tamer couldn't move. The attackers focused all their fury on Wael. His gaze held Tamer's, a silent plea. Then one of the men raised something and brought it down on Wael's head—and the gaze was gone.

"Tamer remained frozen, horrified. He couldn't believe what he'd just seen. Maybe Wael was still alive. Maybe they hit his arm, not his head. Maybe the police would intervene now, end this massacre, fix everything. But none of that happened.

"One of the attackers looked at Tamer. Two others moved toward him but were called off. He stayed motionless, then looked up and realized he was alone. He forced himself up and ran, stumbling down the tunnel toward the door. It was still padlocked. A young man outside was trying to break the chain. Moments later, he managed to crack the lock and unfasten the chain, but the surge of terrified fans behind the gate trampled him and the door flat. Dozens stormed through, stepping over the iron gate and the boy who opened it.

"Tamer made his way forward. There were a thousand young men trying to escape through that single gate. Without thinking, Tamer threw himself over the crowd. He doesn't remember what heads he landed on or how he rolled, but somehow, he reached the exit. He escaped the death trap."

"He survived?"

"Yes. He was the only one of the three who did, with a broken leg, disjointed knee, and a few other fractures. But he lived."

"And Wael and Moheb?"

"Their photos are on the wall at Al-Ahly Club, along with the other 72 murdered kids."

"How horrible."

"Yup."

"Can we pause for a minute? I need to catch my breath."

Amal got up from the bed and walked into the living room. She pulled a cigarette from Omar's pack, lit it, and disappeared. Omar heard the bathroom door close. Then silence. Fifteen minutes later she returned, having washed her face, but the red rings around her eyes were still visible. She curled up on the bed and asked:

"What happened to Tamer after that?"

"He was in and out of hospital for a while. Had two operations to repair his knee and ligaments—enough to walk again, though his leg is still fragile. The surgeries and rehab cost a fortune—thankfully, he had the money. But what broke inside him was far worse than his bones and bank account."

"I can imagine."

"Tamer's rage had no limit—unusual for him, who had always been the soft-spoken, obedient kid. It kind of turned him into a pit of anger, hungry for vengeance. Angry at the security forces—for their negligence, their complicity. Angry at Al-Masry's fans. Angry at a society that produced so many damaged souls. Angry at everyone for moving on as if nothing had happened. Angry even at his fellow Ultras, whom he'd thought too smart and tough to fall into such a trap.

"But he was angriest of all at himself, because he left his friend to die. In the moment that mattered most, he played dead while his friend was being murdered right in front of him. He says he sees Wael's eyes—those pleading eyes—constantly. He blames himself, naturally. Maybe if he'd attacked, the men would've split up and Wael would've lived. Maybe together, they could've fought back. There were possibilities. But what's certain is this: he stayed still and let them kill his friend. And it consumes him."

"He's too hard on himself."

"Or just honest. Tamer swore he wouldn't rest until there was justice. He joined every action the Ultras took, and then some. He let his business collapse. Focused all his energy on tracking the killers, gathering evidence, following the case, protesting, planning revenge.

"During one protest, clashes broke out with the police. He was arrested and released on bail. That became another turning point. His thirst for personal revenge against the police doubled. Eventually, he was arrested again—in a different protest—and sentenced to five years in prison."

"Right, you mentioned that before."

"He was just released two weeks ago, as part of the deal between my father and Colonel Ayman."

"And what happened to his wife? Aya?"

"She joined the bereaved brigade: Aunt Maryam and Layla."

"You're too morbid"

"Me? Why? I didn't make up this story! I didn't kill off all those amazing kids just to impress you with a tragic tale!"

"No, you didn't make it up. But you chose this story—from many others. You spotlighted it. Made it the centerpiece. You're the one telling the stories: you sift through countless events, pick a handful to dwell on—and ignore the rest. You're the narrator, you shape my gaze to what you want me to see. In that sense, your telling doesn't just recount the story—it creates it."

"Fuck you!"

"Ok, very mature!" Amal scoffed.

"How am I supposed to respond? Really? What bright side, exactly, have I ignored?"

"I don't know. I wasn't there. I don't know what really happened. I don't know how Al-Masry fans would tell it. Or the security forces. If they told this story, it would be a different one."

"Go to hell."

"If you say so!"

"This story has only one version. One truth. No debate."

"Omar, just think. Use your brain: it's not just a data warehouse; it has a processor, too, so use it! There are other sides to the story! Even in your version, there's a side you've ignored."

"Fine! Why don't you tell me about the side I've ignored?"

"No, you're the storyteller! I am just pointing out that ..."

"You don't get to point out shit! Do you know what it means to lose your friend? And in this way? Can you imagine how their mothers feel? Wait, I will read it to you. It's online. Listen. This is what Moheb's mother wrote on her page once the shock wore off. Wait, here it is. Listen to this:

You call him a martyr. But don't forget that he is, was, someone's child, someone's flesh and blood and emotions and life. A blurred image on an ultrasound, numbers on a lab report. My glucose levels, my blood type and his father's, the search for a safe hospital, birth plans—natural or cesarean? Complications. The food I had to eat for the baby, for my own health. The things we bought: a crib, diapers, clothes, size 0-3 months, then 3-6, then 6-9, and so on. The first nursing. Did he latch on or not? Would we need formula? Which brand?

He wouldn't sleep. Or slept too much. I worried that he would suffocate if he slept on his stomach, that he would choke on spit-up if on his back or hit his head if on his side. I watched him: he smiled, lifted his head for the first time like he was preparing to rise. I remember his first solids; he spit them out. I had to trick him into eating. I remember when he stood, laughed out loud. Periods when he cried constantly. He was a light sleeper and sometimes I was awake with him all night, through fever, allergies, everything.

As he grew, I had to wonder, should I go back to work or extend my leave? What if I put him into nursery school too soon? Would my mother help, and at what cost to her nerves and mine? When he turned a year old, he had two teeth on his lower gum, and drool always soaking his shirt. Was that normal or do we need another doctor visit? I was always afraid he'd catch another cold.

He stood by himself. Took a step and fell. Then, I spent a year chasing him, trying to stop him from falling, and then he was running, trying to find his balance, to find himself. The chase never ends. Soon enough it was his first day of daycare, and we both cried. And I remember all of the 'firsts': the first time he fed himself—there was food all over his shirt, his chair—everywhere but his mouth. The first book he claimed as his, his first toy, first word, first illness, first healing.

Then he was off to school. He made his first friend, got into his first fight, took on his first hunger strike at home. There was the first time he went out alone—he was with someone we trusted, but still we worried. Soon enough, his first time with friends we didn't know. His first football match, the day he inexplicably decided he was an Ahly fan.

First signs of puberty, and my first realization that he had thoughts and a life apart from us. His father's death came when he was far too young, and I had never-ending anxiety—the guilt of parenting alone. The worry that his father's absence would affect him. Trying to make up for it. Afraid to spoil him. Afraid to be too cold. He turns fourteen, stops talking to us, then 18, and he is back, but different. All those major milestones—and all the quiet ones in between. The everyday, forgotten ones. The ones without names except 'life.' His life. My life with him.

Then a stranger comes along and wipes it all out in a single moment.

After a moment, Amal whispered, "May he rest in peace."
"May we all."
"But what if we told the story from another angle?" she pushed again.
"Why are you suggesting?"
"Imagine, say, Mohamed: a poor farmer, now conscripted in the Central Security Forces. Posted at the stadium. He's not with Ahly or Masry or the Ultras or the revolution or the police. He just wants to finish his service and go home to his village. He's caught in this chaos—flares, fireworks, boys leaping and screaming, then thugs with knives. He's ordered to withdraw. But as he's leaving, he sees a group attacking a young boy, about to throw him off the stands. He breaks rank

and runs to save him."

"Are you working for the Army's propaganda department?"

"Or another story: a young Masry fan, surrounded by Ahly Ultras out for revenge. They beat him so badly he ends up permanently disabled."

"Amal, please shut up. Let what's left of our time together pass peacefully. Is this how human rights activists view it? I swear if I post on Facebook that this is your reaction to the Ultras' deaths, I'd have a mob outside your door within an hour."

"But don't you see? You're threatening me with force. You and your friends are no different from those you condemn. Human rights mean protecting everyone's rights—not just those you love or agree with, but even those you hate and believe to be guilty. It means protecting people from being sentenced in the court of public opinion. And that's exactly what you and your friends are doing. You frame the story, strip out what you dislike or don't understand, then pass judgment. And all that's left is waiting for someone to carry out the sentence."

"Well, you don't have to worry about that. No one carried out any sentence, not one of the trap-setters was charged."

"But you've still judged them."

"I apologize. What do you want now?"

"I want the whole story. I want the stories of the Masry fans and their mothers. The players. The soldiers. The officers. Their families."

"Sure. Next week, inshallah. After your glorious departure, I'll devote myself to truth-seeking and send you a report."

"My point is: your story isn't complete. At least consider that there's more you don't know. Keep room for it. Don't reject it out of hand when fragments come your way."

"Inshallah."

"Now, tell me the rest."

"The rest?"

"What happened to Mai, Wael's girlfriend? And to the three people Moheb, Wael, and Tamer saved in Tahrir

Square?"

"Who?"

"Saeed, Habashy, and Rasha. See how you forget the living and fixate on the dead? You can't see past gloom!"

"Alright, fine. I'll tell you. Mai was taken in by her friend Hend—the one who introduced her to Wael. Hend did her best to support her. But Mai sank into a deep depression. At first it looked like hyperactivity—throwing herself into Ultras events and protests. Then, she had a string of destructive flings. She dated almost every wrong guy imaginable, as if on a mission to wreck herself. Then, she dated Hend's friend, and the two women had a falling-out so bad it split their social circle. And then she left him and dated his friend. And so on. After months of this chaos, she disappeared from everyone's lives. Shut herself in. Deleted her Facebook and Twitter accounts. Total isolation. I heard she got married and moved abroad—but I'm not sure."

"And Rasha and Habashy?"

"I know nothing about Rasha. But I ran into Habashy a few months ago. He still works at the Ministry of Transport and still has the same 800-pound salary. He had a baby girl— said he almost named her 'Tamer' after the man who saved him. His wife, thank God, stopped him."

"And Saeed?"

"No idea."

"And that's it?"

"Yeah! That's the story."

"You have nothing more on them."

"Well, I don't know what's left."

"You could know. You know how to find them. Don't you care what happened to the people your friends saved? Isn't that what remains of them? Couldn't that legacy be part of their story?

"I don't know anything about them."

"Make up a story about them then. Don't you want to be a storyteller? Then invent."

"No."

"Fine, I will. May I?"

"Knock yourself out!"

"Alright, listen. Let's start with Saeed. He came back to the square several times looking for Moheb to thank him. He never found him. The first time he saw him again was in the papers, with the news of the Port-Said massacre. It hit him hard: this boy had saved his life, and now he died the way Saeed himself almost had. He kept repeating it to his wife.

"Then, he started saying he felt like he'd stolen Moheb's life. She got worried. She's a psychologist—she knew where that kind of talk could lead. But she didn't push him. Took the gentler approach. She suggested they visit Moheb's family to offer condolences. He agreed.

"They went to the family home in Nasr City. Slowly, they became close to Moheb's mother and sister. Saeed and his wife practically adopted the sister. He helped Moheb's mother navigate her grief, used his accounting expertise to close Moheb's company and sell it.

"Moheb's mother said her Catholic upbringing taught her to hate the sin and love the sinner—to help the sinner step away from his sin, not punish him for it. So, she decided to use the money they got from the business sale to start an educational center in Port-Said, to provide opportunities to school dropouts and to fight hate.

"Saeed's wife walked with her through the grief until she could carry the memory of her son without it crushing her. Saeed's children became like new children to her."

"Well, thank God, you didn't marry her off to them!"

"Cut the sarcasm. Maybe Rasha married one of Wael's brothers."

"I knew it!"

"Why not? She went to offer condolences, kept visiting, kept in touch. Wael had lots of brothers, as you said. She was young, full of life, looking for a future. Of course it makes sense. One of them fell for her. She for him. They married. It's like Wael gave her to his family before he left."

"And Habashy? Is he getting married, too?"

"Habashy's probably going to end up in prison."

Omar laughed, "Why him?"

"Because he seems gloomy like you!"

"Alright, that's enough. I'm tired. And you're starting to lose it. Let's get something to eat."

"Enough eating. Let's get some sleep. Also, I need to recharge my phone."

"Sleep is good. This is what shitty days are good for."

"This is a shitty day? This is the best day you ever had!"

4

Hend and Bassem
Discover the Three Orifices

Saturday, 7:00 a.m.

He looked at her bare back silently for a while, listening to her breathing, then asked, softly,

"Awake?"

She didn't reply or even stir. He kept staring at her back, at her scattered hair. He decided that he loves her back, her skin, her hair. He gently touched it and repeated the question:

"Amal?"

"Yes?"

"Do you want something to eat? I am a little hungry"

"How many meals do you eat in a day?"

"Be nice, I am your guest. Get up and make me a sandwich or something."

"I'll assume that's a joke. Go to the kitchen and help yourself."

Grumbling, he got out of bed and headed to the kitchen. He felt restless. He'd only slept two hours. He wasn't usually anxious. In fact, he could sleep through just about anything. But sleeping next to a woman, he wasn't used to that. He had never even spent this much time with one, in or outside bed. He never talked that much either. True, he was telling other people's stories, but still. These were his stories too. All these events touched him, directly. And he'd never opened up like this before. Why now, and why to her? Is it because she was leaving, because he'd never see her again? Or is it simply because she was smart, the smartest person he'd ever met—

she was well-read, had lived in many countries, had seen a lot, and he knew she'd understand? Maybe he was just tired of his own silence and needed to speak and she happened to be there and to ask. But would he really never see her again? Or would something happen, like in the movies?

With his plate, he made his way back to the bedroom. She felt him touch her back and jolted:

"Are you going to eat in bed?"

"Do you have a problem with that?"

"Out. Get out of here, now."

She shoved him with surprising insistence, pushing him away along with his plate, where a sandwich of cheese, tomato, and olives shifted and almost fell on the bed. He stood beside the bed, watching her cover her face with a pillow and point toward the living room without looking:

"Go eat there. I don't want ants in my bed."

"What do you care? You're leaving tonight."

"The ants don't know my schedule. Go eat at the table like a human being. And make me a sandwich, too."

He scoffed, picked up his plate, and walked to the kitchen where he made another sandwich. While he worked, he smiled to himself: He had really come a long way! From the Northern Khartoum 'farm' to Amal Mofeed's kitchen in Zamalek at seven in the morning, in boxers, while she was naked in bed? Then he wondered, why couldn't he stay naked, not even in bed? And what were these sandwiches he was making? Since when was he a kitchen guy? How had he ended up following her instructions like this?

He paused, thought about leaving the sandwich and going back, but figured that would make him look even more childish, and carried on.

He liked her kitchen; it was functional, minimalist, clean. Even though he didn't usually like this type of apartment, he was beginning to like this one. It was comfortable. Plenty of open space, not much stuff. Sparse furniture, nothing in the way, everything she had was useful. He didn't feel the usual foreignness he felt in other Zamalek apartments. He knew he didn't belong, that this wasn't a home like any he'd known, but it wasn't alien either. Things here were kind of weightless, just functional and comfortable. He wouldn't mind staying here for few more days. He could live here for a while, actually, or in a place like it, if he had money again.

He carried the second sandwich back to the table and ran into her coming from the bedroom. She walked past him in her stark nakedness, not at all self-conscious, as if that were her natural state. *Well, it kind of is,* he thought. But he still wondered how she got to be that comfortable in her body. Did she always walk around her house naked? How did she live without shame, unlike him, unlike everyone he knew, unlike Eve, banished from Eden? Or maybe like Eve, before the serpent and the apple tree and all that.

She caught his gaze, followed it down to her legs.

"What's wrong with my legs? A bit chubby, right? Prison ruined my body."

"Not at all."

"I'm wide awake now. Is that sandwich really for me? Thank you!"

"I can't sleep."

"Perfect. So why don't you tell me the next story?"

"Alright. But no interruptions and modifications."

"And what's the point of storytelling if I can't interrupt?"

They sat at the table, each with their plate and sandwich. Omar opened his mouth to speak.

"But tell me first, is this story depressing too?" Amal cut in.

"Oh no, it is very cheerful."

"Are you being serious?"

"Do you want a rosy story?"

"I could use one."

"Alright, fine. Hend loved Bassem and he loved her back. They were both eighteen. He was arrested at a checkpoint, held in pretrial detention, and now, it's been ten months of renewals."

"You're a riot."

"Alright, forget that one. Let's switch it up. They loved each other, she got pregnant, and her father killed her."

"Maybe I'll just go straight to the airport."

"Fine, shall we go back to the original story?"

"I'm listening, and recording."

"You're still recording?"

"Yep."

"Why?"

"Just go ahead, leave the technical side to me."

"Ok listen. I will read to you a testimony from a news outlet. It was published on Mada Masr on July 7, 2014:

On December 26, Hend was alone late at night in a secluded, non-residential, street of central Cairo. She remembers that it was icy-cold outside. As she was putting things in a car she had borrowed from a friend, three men appeared from behind and grabbed her. After they grabbed Hend, the three men frogmarched her toward a wall. She says that one man, tall with a sturdy build, did all the talking. He said, 'You've been going around alone a lot these days. I guess that's normal for a street dog like you who likes to be fucked. Tell me you want it. If you don't, I'll put this knife in your pussy,' Hend recalls. 'Then he ripped my leggings open at the crotch with the knife.'

The knife drew blood where it had touched her skin. The man wiped his fingers in the blood and smudged it on Hend's mouth. He handed the knife to the second man, she says. The third was filming using a mobile phone. The first man instructed Hend to get down on her knees. 'He told me to kneel down 'in the place I belong and perform my role,' asking, 'Or is [name of Hend's partner] better than me? Suck me off, and if you bite me, I'll stab you.'

The second man held the knife to her neck. With his other hand he inserted a finger in Hend's anus. 'The first man ejaculated on my face. Then, he forced his penis inside me briefly and asked me which I preferred better. He told me to get up and said that they would send the video to my 'faggot boyfriend'.' Hend says that as the men left her in the street, the first one referenced the 'January 28 queers who take it in all three orifices like [she] did.'

"I've lost my appetite," Amal pushed her half-eaten

sandwich away.

"Wait. The story hasn't even started. That was only the preface."

"Ugh, go ahead."

"The story begins earlier, in 2005. Hend was writing a story about a protest by the Kefaya Movement, when she saw gangs of thugs assaulting female protesters, ripping their clothes, groping them, and so on. She was shocked to her core. She knew sexual harassment and assault was rampant. She had heard about plenty of rape cases. But everything she'd known until then had sounded like individual acts—specific men attacking specific women. What she saw that day was different: impersonal, collective, almost professional. These attackers moved like bulldozers unleashed on a crowd of women, deliberately aimed at crushing them.

"While most reports focused on the identity of the perpetrators, Hend's story focused on the women: What did they do afterward, what did each one do after her clothes were torn, after being dragged by her hair, after being assaulted in public? What did she do once she escaped or was finally left alone? Did she gather her scattered things herself? Did she go home? Did she tell her mother, sister, husband, father—or did she also fear their reaction? Did she decide to pretend she'd been hit by a car or fell off a bus or got dragged down the street by a motorcyclist trying to steal her purse? Or did she collapse into a loved one's arms? How did she spend that night? Did she sleep at all? Did she take sedatives? Did she replay the scene in her head over and over—lying on the asphalt, bruised, half-naked, while assaulting hands groped her, while some thug overpowered her, invaded her?

"And what did she do the next morning? Did she go back to her life as if it had been all a nightmare, or did she talk to someone? And if she did, did it help?

"The attack in 2005 changed Hend's life. She began tracking down the victims of that day's assaults, trying to speak with anyone she could, looking for ways to help. What began as an empathy trip quickly became her life's work. Hend wasn't a therapist. She didn't know much about dealing with survivors of sexual violence—but she learned. In a society that still blames victims—their clothes, behavior, the way they walk—a society that views raping non-virgins as less criminal, since they're 'already fucked,' even the most basic understanding of sexual violence counts as a major step toward better care. That's what Hend offered at first: empathy, emotional support. Then, she started helping survivors find a doctor or therapist. She read more. Gradually, she began helping survivors gather themselves, speak about what had happened, stop blaming themselves, open their hearts, and seek professional help—therapy or legal action.

"This became her full-time passion, on a purely voluntary basis. She didn't create an NGO or join an official group—she was the organization. She did her day job as a journalist while also following news of assaults, tracking down victims and their families, providing doctors, lawyers, support—by phone, through her network, on her own time. Over the years, three things happened: First, Hend became a central figure to dozens of women who had survived sexual violence, a walking archive of resources, connected to everyone in the field. Second, the security services started tracking her: who was she? Who stood behind her? Who was pushing—or funding— her? Third, Hend's heart quietly shattered, bit by bit, day by day, victim by victim—as she listened to story after story of assault and the deep wounds it left.

"I won't dwell on this, you can imagine how it felt to hear these stories straight from the survivors, raw, while they trembled, curled in their beds trying to disappear, or locked in the bathroom and refusing to come out. Hend's heart broke into little pieces, held together only by life's pressure—the need to do a job, to run errands, to deal with people. But when that pressure briefly let up—on a moonlit summer night, in a dark movie theater, or when her face rested against a bus window—tears would flow, seemingly without reason. Or with reason only she knew and chose to ignore.

"This is where Bassem came in. He was a journalist, like her. Young, like her, and from Shubra, like her. I think he and Hend had known each other at school, but their relationship only deepened once they started working together. Bassem was a textbook self-made guy. No one taught him anything. He studied journalism at the Faculty of Mass Communication, but learned nothing relevant there, so he turned to the internet, downloading books and short documentaries about the craft. He taught himself English the same way. Over time, Bassem became quite knowledgeable. He knew all the major journalists around the world, their work, the changes in reporting, media trends, mainstream and alternative outlets, investigative journalism sites and groups. His knowledge went way beyond what he needed for his day job. But it sharpened his instinct, his tools, and taught him what he needed to know to excel at his work.

"In the newsroom, he did what everyone else did, played along. Everyone has bills to pay. But when he submitted mediocre work, he knew it, and secretly longed for a chance to do the job right. He tried a few times. He proposed improvements, pitched ideas. But his bosses reminded him of his place: he was told to remain quiet, do what he was told, and avoid excessive ambition.

"He sometimes submitted high-quality pieces—well-written, multi-angled, researched. That made his editor suspicious: Was he showing off? Shaming his colleagues? Trying to get the attention of the editor-in-chief? It wasn't just his editor, but his colleagues too. After they reacted this way a few times, he got the message: don't step out of line. So, he stepped back. But he still dreamed of a day when he could break rank, or when the whole line might move forward. He waited.

"In the meantime, he fell for Hend. What first caught his eye was her softness. She didn't have a softness that everyone notices, it was not the obvious kind, it was rather like grace. He saw it in her movements; in every step she made. Her smallest gesture of, say, taking a cup of tea from the office boy had a kind of grace that only he saw. Bassem studied her: how she stood, how she walked, how she sat, how she ran for the bus and jumped in it, how she wrote, how she played with her hair, how she adjusted her clothes. He was captivated by this quality he couldn't quite name—a smoothness, a quiet flow that emanated from her core and was reflected in her movement, her speech, her thoughts.

"Don't get me wrong—Hend was not at all fragile. She could stand her ground. But even when she did, she did it with grace. That made her quietly seductive—without trying, without wearing or doing anything in particular, she just radiated femininity.

"Hend fell for Bassem, because he radiated masculinity. The first sign of it, for her, was his integrity—what we call *gad'ana* in Egyptian slang. It's kind of like chivalry, a manliness without machismo, a rough-edged kindness, a boldness and willingness to pay the price if need be. She loved his indifference to petty things, his refusal to get drawn into melodrama. His intelligence. His self-reliance. His humility. His sense of humor. His respect for her. And his quiet awe of her. No one had ever looked at her the way Bassem did. Even when they were discussing something mundane—a newsroom detail, or coverage of a story—his eyes shone with admiration and desire. She felt it, and she loved it.

"It didn't take long for the woman who radiated femininity and the man who radiated masculinity to fall in love with each other. They kind of gravitated toward each other, like two halves completing one another. Then they became inseparable. If you invited Bassem, it was understood Hend was invited too. If she showed up somewhere, he was surely on the way. Hend and Bassem, this was how everyone saw them—together. When the revolution started, they were together in the square. Their tent was the one where Wael first met Mai, remember them?"

"Yes, Wael from Imbaba and Mai the Revolutionary Socialist."

"Exactly. Hend, like Bassem, identified as a leftist—she was 'New Left,' or so she claimed. But the truth was, she was simply a generous friend to everyone. Her work supporting survivors of sexual violence had made her that way—or perhaps it was the other way around. Either way, she became a trusted center for many. In the square, she took it upon herself to ensure the safety of women from harassment and assault. Those were the golden days of Tahrir Square, but they didn't become golden on their own; people like Hend and her friends made them so. She formed small teams to roam the Square, they monitored its entrances and exits, navigated the crowds—stopping or containing harassment before it spread. No one knew how things would unfold in those days, and the square was full of all sorts of people—vigilance was essential. 'Hend's patrols,' as they became known, were welcomed by all, and gradually became more like joyful processions than acts of monitoring—at least at first.

"Things deteriorated quickly, as you probably know. It started with the army's 'virginity tests,' then spiraled into mass sexual assaults orchestrated by 'the unknown party,' including the harassment of the women protesting harassment. It turned into an actual war—the assaulters were an organized, ruthless army. Neither Hend nor her friends understood that at first. For a while, they believed the sexual violence was spontaneous, stemming from the security vacuum or social collapse or chalking it up to the young, repressed and deprived males who saw an opportunity. But the truth proved more brutal than anything they'd imagined. Assaults were carried out by groups, organized and armed, in the middle of streets, and nobody was able to stop them. The more Hend and her comrades intervened, the more they were hurt. Eventually, the women fighting sexual violence became as traumatized as the victims they were trying to help. The burden overtook them. And they began to unravel.

"Hend and Bassem, too, unraveled.

"When the assaults took on that organized, armed form, Bassem asked Hend to pause her anti-harassment work, 'it's futile', he said, 'worse, it's a trap.' 'They're baiting you, whoever 'they' are.' She agreed with his analysis, but she couldn't quit. She couldn't retreat and surrender. To admit defeat would burn her just as badly—if not worse. He tried to understand but couldn't. 'You know you'll be attacked the minute you enter that crowd, in a way that no one can stop. So why would you go there?' Hend would flare up at this line of questioning, go on a tirade, and ultimately leave him with no answer. Gradually, he began to think she had just become addicted to victimhood, that she threw herself into the fire to purge the guilt of having been spared.

"Hend admitted she felt responsible for all of it. She had encouraged women to go out, to challenge sexual harassment and assault. To retreat now felt like cowardice. Bassem lost patience: 'That's nonsense. Everyone should pull out. Do the living kill themselves out of guilt for the dead?' Hend would gaze at him absently and murmur, 'Maybe they should.' And the communication would break down.

"Bassem spoke to her friends about it. Mai told him that he was 'too soft, needed to 'man up.' He was shocked. They argued for hours about feminism, gender, and relationships. In the end, Mai said every relationship involves a power dynamic, and Hend clearly needed to feel his strength. 'Some things are felt, not said,' she told him—and left him even more confused.

"He started to accompany Hend more, like a bodyguard. One evening she discovered, by accident, that he was carrying a pocketknife. They argued that night. They argued for months. Eventually, the burnout that gripped so many had reached them too. When they finally parted, at the end of that year, no one was surprised, certainly not them. Afterward, both Hend and Bassem went through a string of short, failed relationships. In every man, Hend looked for the old Bassem. In every woman, Bassem looked for the old Hend. But they were each searching for a past version of themselves—an image frozen in January 2011 at Tahrir Square. The years that followed drained them to a point where neither could recognize the other. All that was left was the lingering scent of that other, of someone long gone. They were miserable. Their love lives collapsed, perhaps inevitably, and they watched each other from afar. So, it was symptomatic of the police's inefficiency that Hend's assailant referred to 'her faggot boyfriend,' years after they had split.

"Bassem's life was collapsing alongside the collapse of collective dreams of freedom and whatnot. It was hard for him to separate his public and personal life, maybe because he had none. Bassem woke up thinking about the news. He often dreamed about it. He ate breakfast in front of his computer, flipping obsessively through news outlets. On his way to work, he thought about what he read. When his taxi driver was reckless or rude, he didn't just blame the driver, he thought about the failure to enforce traffic laws, about the absence of a proper licensing system, about why Egypt's streets were chaos compared to other countries. Was it culture? Genes? Or just a lack of sensible regulation? His frustration with traffic wasn't just stress—it was despair at state failure.

"At the office, he plunged into endless discussions: 'What's happening?' 'Where are we going?' Conversations that spanned politics, violence, media, the judiciary—every corner of public life. They lasted all day: in his office, the newsroom, conference halls, NGO offices, press briefings, the editor-in-chief's office, and on the phone with sources and friends. They only ended when he fell asleep again, where these issues turned into dreams.

"Whether his work drove him to this obsession, or his obsession led him to this line of work is of little relevance. Practically, the public sphere had become the axis of his life. So, when he went to cover the Maspero protest in October 2011 and saw the crushed bodies of his friends, the trauma hit him like he had been run over by an armored vehicle himself. He spent the next day moving between Maspero, the Coptic Hospital, and the homes of the dead. He detected a silent accusation in the eyes of his friends' parents, perhaps because he had downplayed Coptic rights, because he hadn't acted as a Copt and left that fight to others, to their now-dead sons. Or perhaps simply because he was alive and they were not. No one said anything, but he felt the accusation.

"The armored vehicles that ran over his friends were just the beginning. A long chain of tragedies followed: friends were killed, then more friends, and more still. A month rarely passed without someone he knew falling dead: shot by security forces, by 'the unknown party,' by invisible bullets, or by no bullets at all. Regardless of who and how, they were still getting murdered.

"Death changes us in strange ways. Have you lost a friend your age? It kind of starts with disbelief, then you feel cheated—as though some law of the universe has been broken. People aren't supposed to die in their 20s. But suddenly you realize that they do. They vanish, for real. And you could vanish too, just like that. Sure, we all know life can end anytime, but knowing it is not feeling it. And when that death is murder—by bullets no one fired, sometimes bullets that everyone denies even existed—the cheating feels bigger. The law of the universe hasn't just broken; someone's responsible for it. And you can guess who, but you can't do shit about it. So, you hate them. You wait for the day when you'll see justice. No matter what they say. No matter what they write. You just hate and wait.

"But hatred and anger, as you know, devour their host before anyone else. And Bassem's anger and hatred piled up, day by day, week by week, month by month. With each defeat, his rage deepened. And as his hope faded, so did journalism. The brief taste of freedom vanished. He was back to arguing with his editors about wording, sourcing, timing, relevance— whether something should be published at all. Then the media collapsed entirely into a pit, and the state began purchasing or taking over private outlets. In addition to anger, Bassem also felt shame at his profession, at the way he spent his days. His anger hardened, until it felt like a rock lodged in his chest. It's no wonder Bassem's spirit went out. The wonder is that it took such a long time to die.

"After the assailants had left, Hend sat on the ground, her back against the wall. It's hard to describe what she felt: a mixture of violation and powerlessness, disgust and revulsion at her own body, which had turned into an object, a tool used by men she loathed to humiliate her. She felt a desire to scream, to cry, and to stay composed, all at once. She had a thirst for revenge mixed with despair at the impossibility of exacting it. After some time, she got up, dragging all of that back home. She shut the door of her apartment, dropped everything on the floor, and rushed to the bathroom. She tore off her clothes and stood under the shower, scrubbing her body in a frenzy until her skin hurt. When she could no longer go on, she sat on the floor under the stream of water, sobbing as the water kept falling. She stayed like that until she dozed off or lost consciousness. When she regained consciousness, the hot water had run out and the shower was pouring cold water on her. She turned it off, dried herself, cleaned her wounds, applied ointments and creams to sooth them. She rinsed her mouth with antiseptic for the tenth time. Then, she dressed and went to Bassem's apartment.

"There was no hesitation on Bassem's part. When she told him what had happened, the only thought that came to his mind was how to avenge her, and how to ensure nothing like this could ever happen to her again. The first task, however, was to help her survive this ordeal. But how would he care for a caregiver? How would he comfort someone who knows every page of the comforting handbook? Knowing the approach made caregiving hard, made it feel like a script. Bassem knew this is how she'd feel if he tried, so he called one of her friends instead. That friend stepped in with dedication and tact, but she also told Mai, the Revolutionary Socialist whose friendship with Hend had ended months ago. When Mai learned what happened, she immediately went to see Bassem.

"Mai found Bassem home alone—he had just returned from Hend's place. He seemed angrier than she had ever seen him—and confused. Mai tried to calm him down, saying people often focus on the survivor—Hend in this case—and forget that those close to them are also traumatized. When he said he felt guilty, she urged him not to be too harsh on himself. 'Hend isn't a child,' she said. 'None of us are. We all pay the price for our choices, and we know it. It is not your burden to carry.' He objected, she explained more, he cried, she held him, and one thing led to another. So, when Hend had a panic attack in the middle of the night, couldn't reach Bassem by phone, and came to his apartment using her old key, she found him in bed with Mai.

"There was a meeting of their friends planned for the next

morning to discuss how to respond to the assault on Hend. The tension in the air was palpable. Everyone thought it was the result of the attack, except Hend and Bassem. Neither of them had slept at all. The night was truly brutal, with an avalanche of insults and fighting. Hend was beyond shocked to find Mai in his bed. She asked him how he could be so insensitive—and how he could stoop so low, pointing to Mai. Bassem couldn't understand Hend's reaction. After all, they'd broken up a while ago. 'And why do you need to insult her?' he asked. Hend scoffed, saying Mai was 'too cheap to deserve an insult,' to which Mai returned the favor, and both of them went into a tirade of detailed insults. In the middle of it, Hend looked at Bassem disparagingly, calling him a 'faggot,' just as the assailing officer had. Bassem was speechless. Mai smirked and murmured 'cunt!' which unhinged Hend entirely. She flung the nearest object at Mai, which happened to be a bottle of red wine. Luckily, the bottle missed Mai's head and landed on the floor instead. Bassem tried to get Mai to leave, but she refused. He tried to calm Hend down, but she wouldn't. And so, the three carried on the mutual abuse until morning. Mai left first, refusing to attend the meeting. Then, Basem and Hend left to meet the rest of the group. It would probably have been better to postpone, but there was no time.

"Bassem and Hend sat apart, avoiding eye contact. The others didn't fully understand what was happening but refrained from prying. The meeting proceeded. The human rights lawyers recommended reporting the incident to the prosecutor—not to seek justice, which was unlikely, but to document the assault and preserve the legal case. Still, they agreed that holding the perpetrators accountable, or even deterring them in the future, was all but impossible. These assaults were part of a systematic policy, not individual misconduct that might be punished if exposed.

"The journalists suggested raising the case in the media and making it a matter of public concern. But they, too, conceded that while this would spotlight the assault, it wouldn't bring justice or deter future attacks. The radical revolutionaries proposed personal revenge, since Hend claimed to know the perpetrator's name. They argued this was the only path forward in the absence of legal avenues. Bassem found himself drawn to the idea, and the more he considered it, the more it animated him.

"The plan was simple. Hend would call the officer, appear broken, accuse him of ruining her life, but at the same time leave the door open for a conversation. He would likely tell her it was her fault; she challenged the security apparatus and thought herself a revolutionary leader. She would respond with controlled vulnerability, prompting him to suggest she cooperate in exchange for protection. She would then set a time and place to meet—somewhere public, but secluded, where Bassem and his friends would ambush him and settle the score. If he suggested to meet her somewhere private, she would offer her place. Again, Bassem and the others would be waiting. The plan wasn't airtight. He might not take the bait. He might just hang up. Or not suggest meeting. Or suggest a place of his choosing. But they wouldn't know unless they tried.

"After some discussion, they decided to go ahead with the revolutionaries' plan. If it failed, they'd think of something else.

"Hend made the call, but it was inconclusive. She started by insulting him, and he insulted her and hung up. The next day, she sent him a text, blaming him for destroying her life. She added that he was wrong about her: she wasn't the loose woman he thought she was. And her 'boyfriend,' Bassem, was actually her ex-husband. They only kept it secret because Bassem was Christian. Now he had raped her, and everything was ruined. He called her back, less hostile this time. She seized the moment, wept, played the broken woman. After a few calls over ten days, he set a meeting at a café in Nasr City. She met him there, stayed in character. They met twice more in public places. She continued with the fragile, sad character. Then, he invited her to his home. She agreed. But two days before the meeting, he canceled—his wife had returned early from the coast. So, she simply invited him to her place. He agreed.

"Everything happened quickly that night. Hend lived on the top floor of a tall building, with a large terrace on Ahmed Abdel Aziz Street. The officer arrived on time, looked smart and polite, and went straight to the terrace as she had suggested. Bassem and three friends stormed the terrace and attacked him. A fierce struggle broke out. After a few minutes, as the group overpowered him, the officer drew his gun and aimed it at the attackers. Everybody froze. But Bassem lunged, trying to knock the gun from his hand. The officer twisted, dodging Bassem's full-body charge. Bassem hit the terrace wall, seemed to steady himself, but then lost his balance and fell. Eleven floors. He died instantly.

"Hend collapsed again. Her friends took turns staying with her, worried that she would try to commit suicide. The officer called and threatened her viciously, then told her she was too low to merit further attention. He warned her: if she took one step against him, he would wipe her and her friends out with the stroke of a pen. After that, she withdrew into her private grief. Her friends withdrew into mourning. And that was the end of the story."

"I'm going to wash my face."

Amal got up and went to the bathroom. A few minutes later, she returned. Omar was still sitting on the bed, staring blankly. Amal started:

"No. No. I object to this story. You're truly dark"

"Me? Dark? You were thrown in jail for organizing governance workshops!"

"I don't believe all of that actually happened. So much of it doesn't make sense."

"Really? How so?"

"It doesn't make sense for Bassem to do any of that. The whole avenger role doesn't suit him. And why does he fall from the eleventh floor? That's melodrama. It would've been easier, and more likely, for the officer to be the one who falls. Or gets thrown."

"Ah, I see. But even if the officer had fallen, his colleagues would know he was meeting someone. The investigation — call logs, surveillance—would lead straight to Hend and the others. They'd all end up in prison for years. Bassem might even be executed for orchestrating it."

"Great. So, in both versions Bassem dies and Hend and their friends get crushed?"

"Exactly."

"Then why pursue revenge in the first place?"

"What else could they do?"

"Will you let me rewrite the story?"

"What would you change this time?"

"I want to change how Hend and Bassem respond to the assault."

"Ah ha!"

"No revenge. They don't try to trap the officer or hurt him. Bassem's too smart for that. He understands that sexual violence is a weapon in a political conflict. It's not personal. Even if individuals commit the act, punishing one won't stop the next. Hend knows this too, at least in her mind—she's worked with victims. So, with the help of their friends—who should also know better than to believe in personal vengeance—they'll come up with something different. Something that confronts sexual violence as policy. Something that protects victims instead of setting out on a self-destructive crusade."

"And what's this genius plan?"

"Patience. Work with me. You've been talking for hours. Now it's your turn to listen."

"Be my guest."

"What did the officer say to Hend? That she takes it in all three openings?"

"Orifices"

"Fine. Hend will use those three orifices as openings to purge the poison he put inside her.

"The first opening: purging the shame. She goes public. She tells her story. It's the first step to healing. Coming forward breaks the shame; it shifts blame to the perpetrators. She posts the story on Facebook, say, and then something miraculous happens. Other women start writing too. Dozens. The post becomes a book of Egypt's sexual sorrows. The collective act of testimony starts to heal the survivors. But it also begins to shift the public. Once there are ten, twenty, a hundred stories, people can't dismiss it anymore. Not even the regime. A lone victim can be blamed. People will always try to shame the victim; even other women do—because it protects them from thinking 'it could be me.' Men find it easier to believe this happens only to 'bad girls.' But if the stories keep coming, if the numbers swell, society will have to confront it. And the regime, even in its tyranny, will have to flinch. That's the first pathway. Hend will be the one who opens it."

"Fine. Even though she already gave her testimony to Mada Masr and none of this happened."

"That was anonymous. This time it's her real name, her real face. You said she was well-known, didn't you? That's the difference. Not just recounting the facts, but standing behind them, unashamed.

"The second opening is connected: documentation. Hend and Bassem listen to the lawyers, file official complaints. And they push other victims to do the same. They know it won't bring justice. But it records the crimes. It builds a case. It helps victims recover. And someday, it could matter. If there will ever be justice, it will have to start with a record."

"Okay, can you wrap it up? I'm starting to doze off."

"Be patient. The third opening might wake you up. Hend reclaims all three orifices, their ownership, their meaning. She and every woman who's been assaulted. Sexual violence does two things: it makes you feel powerless, and it breaks your relationship with your body, with your own sexuality. Hend will undo that. She'll reclaim her body and sexuality—her three orifices, as the officer put it. She and others, those he called 'the revolutionary whores,' will say loudly, with words and with actions, that these bodies are theirs, their orifices belong to them, and giving access to them is a choice they make. They choose when, how, and who gets that access. No one else. Hend will do exactly what the officer accused her of—take it in all three—but only from someone she desires. That's the reclaiming. If she wants to open her orifices—to a husband, a lover, a partner—it's her decision. She'll enjoy herself as she wishes, when she wishes, with whomever she wishes. She will take back what they tried to steal. She'll found a movement—with a website—to teach women how to enjoy their bodies, their three orifices, without shame."

Omar was silent; he didn't quite know how to respond.

"What's wrong? Did I lose you?"

"No. I've just lost hope in you."

"Why?"

"Because what you're saying is all theory. And offensive."

"Why?"

"I'm telling you about a woman who was raped. Humiliated. Broken. By the state that's supposed to protect her. Don't you grasp the scale of what she went through? The depth of the wound?"

"I do."

"Then stop with this nonsense."

"Alright."

He looked away again.

"So now what?" She asked.

"We eat. Or sleep. Or you go catch your flight."

"Or we set ourselves on fire and end it."

"No fires. No melodrama, you don't like it. Sleep. As they say in the army: shitty days are good for bed."

"Brilliant. All brilliant solutions."

"They're not solutions. I never said they were. Be honest with yourself for once: there are no solutions. Don't pretend. This isn't a country. We're not people. You're not human. I'm not. None of us are. This is all farce. So, stop making up fake solutions."

"You know, if you got shot in the eye right now, you'd feel pain like never before. You'd scream, stumble around the room. If I tried to help, I'd hurt you more, and you'd yell that it's pointless, that you've lost your eye. But that wouldn't be you talking. That would be the pain. That part of you. The wounded part. It's natural, but irrational. It's not thinking. You're like a lab rat. They shock you and you react, which is exactly what they want. They hit you so you hit back. They rape you to break your spirit, and you break. They drown you in filth, so you give up. Where is your mind? Where's your thinking? Your agency? Where's your effort to keep going despite the injury? Your feelings are hurt, but reason is supposed to weigh them, to see the bigger picture."

"Your words are so cold, and abstract, and rehashed."

"All thinking is theory. That's what thinking is. And everything is rehashed. Pain. Wounds. Tyranny. Defeat. And also love. Joy. Beauty. Victory. Everything is a repetition. Life itself is a fucking repetition. We just choose from the same old things. That's our lot. We weren't the first ones here."

"You're not from here."

"On the contrary, I am so from here. But I don't give in. That's the difference between us."

They stared at each other. Omar was the first to speak.

"You can only say this because you're safe. You're sitting on the shore, with a boat waiting. You get to say these things from your beach. Your self-help slogans assume we're in a society of humans. Look around you—this is a swamp. And these aren't people. They're mutants. There are no solutions because this is what we are. Maybe once we had a chance. But that's over. We're falling. So, stop trying to choreograph the way we collapse."

"That's what the hopeless always say. The unimaginative. This revolution, none of it could've happened if you were right. If every victim just licked their wounds and cursed their luck instead of inventing a way to fight back."

"And look where that got us."

"It got us here."

"Great. And it's nearly nine a.m. and the light's bothering me. Let me go back to sleep."

"Sure. But first I want to show you a practical demonstration of what I meant. Maybe it'll help you explain it better to your friend."

"I don't follow."

Amal smiled, pulled him toward her, and began to kiss him. He hesitated, lips stiff, but then began to yield. She turned around so that her mouth could reach his penis. Omar, nervous, wasn't aroused. She touched his penis gently with her fingers, then her lips, and asked him to kiss her pussy. He hesitated. She moved it closer to his mouth, held his fingers and guided them to her anus. His penis quickly hardened, she took it in her mouth, slowly. His tongue, increasingly absorbed, thrust into her pussy, while his finger pressed deeper into her anus. She stopped him gently and turned around. With care, she guided his penis into her pussy, kissing him intensely, her tongue deep in his mouth, meeting his. His finger stayed in her anus as his penis penetrated her. She moved his fingers slowly to match the rhythm of his penis. They continued for several minutes, until she gasped and stopped. She gazed into his eyes, pulled his penis out of her and held it in her hand. Then, gently, with her eyes fixed in his, slid it inside her ass. As he penetrated her, she put his finger on her clit, guiding his movements. They pushed together, with Omar hardening more inside her and his fingers moving around her clit. Their eyes locked. She leaned and kissed him hard while they both came with a loud, long scream.

5

Habiba and Shadi
Reach the Morgue

Saturday, noon.

She looked at him intently:

"Awake?"

No answer. She reached out, her fingers combing through his hair, trailing down his neck and shoulders, pausing at his arms—she liked his arms—then along the length of his back. He turned his head and found her watching him.

"What is it?"

"Hungry?"

"Yes."

"Let's go out for breakfast."

"Where?"

"Zooba."

"Why go? We could just order in."

"I like it there."

"Why go all that way to sit on a sidewalk? We can do that downstairs"

"Oh, very funny. I like everything about Zooba. It was our favorite—Chris and I."

"Well, Chris isn't here now. And I don't like sitting on sidewalks."

"Don't you want a change of scenery? A bit of air?"

"I do. But I don't have the energy. I'd rather stay in bed. What time is it?"

"Noon. Want the usual? Fava beans, falafel, eggs, et cetera?"

"Anything. I'll eat whatever you want to eat."

110

"How gracious of you. Anything else?"

"No."

He lay there a while, irritated for no clear reason. It happened often. He tried to pin down the source. He'd been asleep, dreaming. Then he woke to her voice, breakfast. All of that was fine. Ah, it was the time. Noon. Time had passed. But why should that bother him? Did he want her lying here with him, listening to his stories forever? Did he like the game, having the attention of this confident beauty? Was he already missing her? Nonsense. She'd be gone by evening, and he'd never see her again. So, what did it matter?

He considered leaving early. Why wait for her flight? Why the airport ride? Why not just leave now? He shut his eyes, pretending to drift back to sleep. Then her voice called from the other room:

"Don't just lie there. Do something useful! Go take a shower!"

"Yes, Mom."

"I'm disappearing for twenty minutes. Don't run away."

"I won't. I'll probably fall asleep."

"Peace."

"Got music?"

"The speakers are on the table. Connect your phone. Is it charged?"

"Yes. Thanks."

Once the bathroom door clicked shut, Omar got up, synced his phone to her speakers, and turned the volume up. Fairuz filled the room. He leapt out of bed and headed to the second bathroom. He liked the idea of having a second bathroom. It was one of those small luxuries you never think of until you have them. The shower products also impressed him—so many different kinds of soap, shampoo, oils, creams, lined up like soldiers in bright bottles. All this? For what? He picked up each one, studied the labels. She'd been in prison, so where did all this come from? Would she leave it all behind?

At home, they had one bar of soap and maybe a shampoo bottle, usually empty. He'd wash his hair with water or with soap until someone remembered to restock. He stood under the hot water so long the steam fogged the room and the mirror gave up. When he finally turned the shower off and stepped out, Fairuz was still singing:

He showed up and asked if April had knocked.
I hid my face, and the house flew away with me...
He made himself a cup of Arabic coffee.
Still on my mind, sweet and proud—
basil blooming on a rooftop high...

Omar sipped slowly, lit a cigarette, and stood by the window. The quiet of Zamalek on a Saturday morning. He didn't want to admit it, but it was pleasant. He'd trained himself to hate wealthy neighborhoods, probably as a means of resisting their temptation. But Amal wasn't rich, not like the other people he knew from Zamalek. She was like him, more or less. Just smarter, more resourceful, and American. She'd worked hard and landed a good job. That could've been him, if his father hadn't taken him to Sudan, or if Tamer's company hadn't collapsed. But then again, Aunt Maryam and Layla were tied to Bein El-Sarayat. They wouldn't have left it even if the company were still running. But it wasn't, and now he was driving a taxi, and an old one at that.

But what if Amal weren't flying out tonight? What if he'd met her sooner, really gotten to know her at one of those workshops maybe, a few years ago? Would anything be different? Probably not. They'd have walked past each other— they were headed down different paths at different speeds. Neither would have stopped. But what if they had stopped, would they have clicked? He shook the idea out of his head, no point to that now.

Still, what would happen now? He answered himself in his head: She'll come out of the other bathroom. We'll eat breakfast, talk more, maybe have sex one last time, then I'll take her to the airport. The end. He told himself this firmly, like a parent preparing a child to leave the playground. She appeared wrapped in a large towel. He didn't notice her. She stood watching him, intrigued by the way he stared into space.

"Hello, there."

He blinked, then smiled gently. She looked at him—further

intrigued by his unusual smile—and walked past. He reached for her waist; she swerved and kept walking toward the bedroom.

"Make coffee. And get us some cold water. And chop some tomatoes. Breakfast is on the way."

He wandered into the kitchen, did nothing, returned to the window and lit another cigarette. There was something oddly domestic about all this. He scolded himself: What's gotten into you? Stop it. He stubbed out the cigarette and went back to the kitchen, if only to kill time before she returned. Fairuz was still singing. He turned the volume down by half. Waited by the window. She came out wearing an orange t-shirt and bright green shorts. Her hair was wet, trailing down her back. He looked at her and thought, she is beautiful. She noticed his look but said nothing.

"Where's my stuff?" she asked, nodding toward the table.

When he asked what she meant, she said,

"Where's the coffee, the water, and tomatoes?"

"What's the rush?"

She didn't answer, just walked to the kitchen. He followed. She handed him the water and pulled the tomatoes from the fridge. He began making coffee. Then Fairuz started singing Ana w Shadi.

"Where are you going?" she asked.

"To change the song."

"Why?"

"I don't like that one."

"Ana w Shadi?"

"You know the song?"

"Of course. I just never paid attention to the words."

"One moment"

"No, don't change it. Tell me the lyrics."

"I'd rather not."

"What? Why?"

"Just bad memories."

"Ah, a new story. Shall I record?"

"No."

"Please?"

"No."

"Why not?"

"Because. Do you want to start the day with misery?"

"As if you offer anything else. Fine, just tell me the lyrics."

"Okay."

"Thanks. From the top."

He stood, restarted the track, and began to translate:

Long ago, when I was little,
there was a boy
who came from the fields.
I would play with him.
His name was Shadi.
Shadi and I sang together,
played in the snow, ran in the wind.
We wrote on stones ... tiny stories,
and waved to the breeze.
Then one day the world caught fire—
people against people, trapped in this life.
The fighting came closer to the hills,
Shadi ran to watch.
Afraid, I called out to him:
"Where are you going, Shadi?"
[...]
The snow came and went,
Twenty times, the snow came and went.
I grew up, but Shadi stayed small,
Still playing in the snow.

"Are you Shadi?"

"No. I'm not gone yet!"

"Then who's Shadi? Is he dead? Come on, tell me. Here's the phone, ready to record."

"Shadi's a friend, and no he is not dead. He's the son of Mohamed the driver, the one who leased my dad's taxi for the past two years."

"And who is Mohamed the driver?"

"A driver from Fayoum. My father met him by chance during one of his taxi shifts. Mohamed had a son and a daughter; he drove a beat-up pickup for a living. Fayoum doesn't offer much. Poor town. Everyone is either living in abject poverty, or poor but pretending not to be. Work only comes during harvest season, and even then, it's mostly favors—helping neighbors, relatives. You're lucky if they cover gas, most of the time they repay you in kind, or in kindness. Life in trickles.

"Mohamed's kids were growing up. He would need money soon to marry his daughter off. His son, Shadi, got into university; he was smart, quick—too sharp to waste in a pickup truck. But college is expensive. Mohamed hates Cairo, but you go where you can earn your bread. He started working as a private driver but couldn't make it last. The pay was low, the hours long, and they treated him like shit."

He paused. Amal waited, arms folded, eyebrow raised. Omar went on.

"So, he quit and switched to taxi driving. That's when he met my father. They were sitting in a café—one of those places where drivers hang out between shifts. My father liked him. Mohamed wasn't complaining, just telling his story, and when my father offered some comfort, Mohamed nodded and thanked God for what he had. He said life's hard, sure, but that's just how it is. He was always kicking, always moving. My dad liked that. They exchanged numbers. One day, Mohamed called. Asked if he wanted someone to work the other taxi shift. My dad said no at the time. But later, when he got arrested, he remembered him. He gave Mohamed's number to Layla and told her to lease the taxi to him. So she did."

He stopped to sip his coffee, glanced at her, then continued:

"Mohamed moved into Bein El-Sarayat. It was easier that way. Rent was cheap, and the neighborhood is close to the university where his son, Shadi, studied agriculture. And close to us. So, he could pick up and drop off the taxi without wasting time. Layla and Aunt Maryam also liked the idea—having a man nearby.

"He left his daughter and wife in Fayoum but visited them frequently. Shadi stayed with him in Cairo and became my first real friend."

"What about Tamer?"

"Tamer's my cousin. Shadi's my friend. I've always been quiet. I don't like talking, I don't like company. It takes time for me to open up."

"Really?"

"Really. But I felt at ease with Shadi from the start. Perhaps because we had similar backgrounds. Although we made different choices, we both grew up in almost the same conditions: families of devout believers who kept their distance from anyone unlike them. The jihadi group I was raised in was a closed, self-contained world: women, children, men, elders, youths, fighters, emirs, Quranic school, playgrounds, sports, drills in combat—all of it contained within the 'North Khartoum Farm.' Our contact with the outside world was nonexistent. Shadi's family was almost the same, living in a village near Fayoum, among conservative, religious neighbors—mostly members of the Muslim Brotherhood or other Islamist groups.

"When we met, neither of us had ever been to the cinema, or even watched a film on television. You may find that strange, but it's true. Neither of us had ever spoken with a girl alone or even exchanged words with one who wasn't a relative. Neither of us had seen a woman's body, except in pictures. Neither of us had touched a woman. Neither of us had read a book beyond the religious texts, the stories of the prophets, and schoolbooks. Neither of us had listened to a song, except by chance, in a microbus when a driver lingered too long on the wrong station. Neither of us had seen the sea. Neither of us had traveled alone. Neither of us had been in a discussion on anything outside the consensus of the community."

"Oh, sweetheart!"

She hugged him. He stiffened, kept talking while her arms were around him.

"More than all that, neither of us had a mother. Shadi's mother was killed. She had been shot by police during a raid back in the '90s. They were after terrorists. Some said it was her fault—she walked into a crossfire after being warned. Some said otherwise. Either way, she was killed and Shadi was raised by his father, the pickup driver, who remarried and had another daughter.

"His stepmother was kind. She tried not to interfere. Tried to care for him as her own child. But something was missing, and he, like me, didn't know what it was. That was the glue between us, I think. That sameness. Of course, there were differences, too. People say I'm hostile. Shadi's the opposite. He's open, generous, soft-spoken. He had this gift of making hard things sound easy. Like magic. He kept his distance from people, just like me, but with no friction. I watched him, tried to learn. I failed. I always end up fighting. He never did.

"We gravitated toward each other. Started trying things, new things. People. Places. Books. Films. Ideas. Politics. Girls.

"Shadi wanted to be a farmer."

"A farmer?"

"Yeah. Who dreams of that, right? But he did. His family were landless peasants. They worked land they never owned. His grandfather fled Upper Egypt decades ago, without a penny to his name, and ended up in Fayoum by chance. There, he found a bit of stability. He married a farmer's daughter, had kids. None of them ever owned land. Just laborers, all the way down. His uncle saved enough in Saudi to buy a few feddans—half arid—and tried to work it. Shadi's father turned away from that life and became a driver, like I told you.

"And now, Shadi wanted to be a farmer, or more accurately he wanted to build a farm. He said agriculture had evolved everywhere, and his farm would be much more than an ordinary patch of cultivated land. First, he wanted to grow flowers and traditional medicinal herbs. He planned to raise livestock and bees. But more than any of that, he wanted to turn the place into a retreat for anyone seeking a stay in the countryside. He said the model already existed: modest chalets with basic comforts set in the middle of farmland, nothing in sight but open fields. Guests could rent them by the day or the week, even take part in the work if they wished to live the rural life completely.

"He wasn't making this stuff up, he insisted—resorts like this existed all over the world and were thriving. If you asked him how he'd get the land, how he could possibly grow flowers and herbs in a place as unforgiving as Fayoum, or where the money would come from, he'd just laugh and say: 'every problem has a solution.' Modern irrigation and agricultural techniques made almost anything possible, and what wasn't possible today might be tomorrow. Egypt had plenty of land. All he needed was the right training and a small amount of startup capital, maybe a loan. Maybe he would find a team of other dreamers like him, with nothing but their ambition. He had more elaborate ideas, too—about distribution and marketing, the type of workers, life on the farm. I used to tease him, tell him his dream sounded like somewhere between Thomas More's *Utopia* and Bin Laden's farm north of Khartoum. Shadi would laugh and say it would be an agricultural Silicon Valley. 'Just wait,' he promised, 'until I finish my degree and find the right crew.'

"Shadi is the only person who knows nearly everything about me, and I think I know almost everything about him. I told him how I gradually lost my faith at that farm north of Khartoum, and how deeply I came to hate all Islamist groups. He understood, even though he didn't agree. Shadi thought I was an atheist. That's not quite right. I'm just not interested in the subject. Shadi also had doubts. He no longer believed in God the way he was taught, but he couldn't say for sure God didn't exist either. But unlike me, he couldn't let the matter go. 'We need to find answers. I need certainty,' he'd repeat every time the topic came up. I'd ask, 'What if there is no certainty?' He'd shrug and say, 'Then we're lost.' I'd tell him we've been lost for ages. That was the end of it for me. But he kept looking. He kept sending me books, links to websites, debates, long threads of philosophical sparring.

"I don't think Shadi's a believer. He isn't. But he just can't admit it—not even to himself. Sometimes I'd challenge him: 'How could God, if He exists, punish us for using the minds He gave us?' At that, he'd retreat into the typical arguments about using reason only within boundaries, about the temptations of the devil and so on. I'd argue that all that depends on accepting the original premise, which requires reason in the first place. And around and around we'd go.

"Don't get me wrong. Our friendship wasn't just a late-night seminar on theology. We talked about everything. We discovered Cairo together, like two aliens dropped from another planet. We discovered TV shows we'd never seen, plays, old movies, from the seventies, eighties, nineties, songs, novels, books. We devoured it all, without order or filter.

"Then came the revolution, and it blew everything open. The streets, the people, the chaos and hope, the art and violence. I, the recluse, met people of every kind. Shadi kept to his Islamist circles—jihadists, Salafis, Muslim Brothers, friends and neighbors of Brothers, former Brothers. I found them unbearable, especially when they tried to be funny. But Shadi always tried to explain their political evolution, how the Islamic movement was at heart a fight for freedom. Our different views didn't touch the core of our friendship. Neither of us belonged to any political faction. He understood the Islamists better than anyone I knew. I was trying to understand everyone else. We lived in downtown Cairo, our days and nights a constant blur of meetings, protests, rallies, street clashes, artistic productions, friendships, flings, betrayals. And then Habiba appeared.

"There was nothing special about Habiba. She looked like any number of veiled university girls you'd pass without a second glance. She was neither tall nor short. Not thin, not fat. Her figure was always hidden beneath her clothes—which were usually in faded colors. She was neither stylish nor awkward—somewhere in between. Her eyes never really met yours. She moved quickly, as if she was trying not to be seen. Her voice was barely audible when she spoke. Her gaze downward, swallowing half her words."

"And Shadi? What does he look like?"

"He's slim, average height. His temples are a little sharp. He has light skin and curly black hair. He has a neutral face, neither smiling nor frowning, and a trimmed goatee. His eyes protrude slightly, always alert, full of thought."

"And he's soft, a bit?"

"Soft?"

"I mean gentle."

"Kind. Polite. But he can take a strong stand, usually online, through emails or tweets, and then stick to it."

"Okay. And Habiba? What was she doing with her life?"

"She was a first-year sociology student. She'd wanted to study English literature, but the college rules didn't allow 'her kind' in, so she ended up in sociology, which she didn't know much about, and didn't learn much about either. She was poor, from Kafr Tohormos. Devout. Kind. Shadi and I had crossed paths with her a few times without me noticing. The fourth time, he nodded at her. I asked who she was, and he said we'd seen her before at different events. Then, she disappeared again until one day he said, 'there's something going on.' I was surprised. She didn't seem like Shadi's type, but he was completely smitten. He went on about the divine light in her face, the way her eyes pierced his soul, how she finished his sentences, how she understood what he felt before he said it. All the things only the lovestruck can see. I didn't see any of that, but I understood: my friend was in love. That was that. I congratulated him.

"They clicked instantly, as if each had been waiting for the other. Shadi told her about his doubts, but she downplayed them. When he said he wasn't sure he believed in God anymore, she laughed and told him he was a Muslim, a true believer even if he didn't believe so! After all, doubts, she said, don't cancel faith. Even the prophets had them."

"So, he dropped his doubts and followed the first girl who smiled at him?"

"Don't be nasty! Can I finish? Ask your questions after I'm done."

"Fine."

"She was honest, told him how difficult her situation was: they had no money, many siblings, her mother worked a menial job, her father was ill. They rented an apartment, and she took small gigs to help her family. And Shadi loved her more for it.

"I don't know how to explain the effect they had on each other—you'd have to meet them to understand. Shadi became better. As if something inside him finally came together. He was calmer, more focused, more patient, more present. He smiled more. Helped more. Understood more. Grew bolder. Nothing about him got worse. He didn't ditch our friendship. Didn't do any of the pathetic things guys do when they have girlfriends. He didn't hide his questions for her sake. On the contrary, he searched harder, for real answers, with more confidence. Does that answer your question?"

"In a way. But that's what I suspected. He shelved his doubts for the only girl who paid him attention."

"You're really mean! No, of course he didn't. Anyway. Habiba was really a sweet girl. Even I warmed to her eventually. She always acted like Shadi's lawyer, but without ever trying to isolate him from anyone. They were like a perfect match, a natural match. It was clear to all of us that they would eventually get married and build a life together as soon as the world let them."

"And of course nothing physical happened between them."

"No, nothing physical. Habiba's religious and moral convictions were stronger than everything else, including her feelings. They spent a whole year debating whether she would allow him to hold her hand. In the second year—the year of hand-holding—she let him grasp her whole hand but never interlace their fingers. That, according to her, opened a door to something greater. So, he held her hand, just like that, unmoving, until she pulled hers away. That's how it went. Their feelings, of course, were far stronger than any of those restrictions."

"That's a textbook case of sublimation. Psych 101."

"Whatever. Shadi's desire for her—his love—was overwhelming. He couldn't control it. It was enough for him to say 'I love you' on the phone, and for her to reply in kind, five or six times, and that alone would make him come. She, too. Believe me. I heard it once myself, from the room next door."

"I believe you."

"But you're laughing. Maybe you don't get it. Maybe that's

the difference between two cultures."

"Stick to your story. Leave the cultural theory aside."

"All right. That's how they were. In fact, Shadi respected her more because of that. He was, after all, a conservative guy, and would never marry a girl who slept with him before marriage. His doubts about religion didn't mean he'd shaken off the morality he was raised with. So, they both abided by these rules, and both felt guilty after their 'heated' phone calls. But it was a guilt they didn't hold against each other.

"As I said, Habiba became part of our common life. She was with him all the time, in the university, the art spaces, the protests. She wasn't a member of any Islamist group, and neither was Shadi. But she believed, with a quiet certainty, that Islam offered the most just and complete framework for both private and public life. She disagreed with this or that group on this issue or that method. She found them rigid, sometimes backward, often off-putting in their style. She steered clear of their interpretations, mocked their confusion of tradition with revelation, but in the end, she saw salvation and a future in that path. In a way, she was the best kind of Islamist someone like me could ever find. And she'd say I was the best kind of secularist an Islamist could hope for. As for Shadi, he continued his search for certainty, while his heart quietly remained in Habiba's orbit.

"That was our balance, until Shadi graduated in the summer of 2012—and began building the dream."

"The farm? He really started it?"

"He did. He pulled together a crew: ten young people, fresh graduates of agriculture, law, commerce, and Habiba. They loved the idea and had nothing better to do. They drafted a comprehensive proposal and submitted it to the government, asking for fifty feddans to launch the project. In June, they met with two ministers, who approved and signed off on it. The crew walked out of the meeting beaming. One of the minister's chiefs of staff promised to fast-track the paperwork."

"And?"

"And then nothing. The bureaucracy swallowed the

project. One engineer after another, one department head after the next, one undersecretary, then another, then committee after committee, then nothing. It was absurd. A Brotherhood government, the minister on board, and yet nothing got done. Shadi said the bureaucracy was a machine that can take any instruction and shred it until nothing's left. I asked, 'can't the minister just give an order to speed it up?' And he'd say, 'Sure. They get the orders. Then they refer it to a committee to study some aspect. Or pass it to the other ministry for some formality. It has to be legally sound, or this director won't sign, or that division head, or the legal advisor. And so on.' So, nothing happened.

"Shadi's father, Mohammad, said the whole thing needed a bribe—a 'sweetener'—to the officials at the ministry and in the governorate where the land is. He said they wouldn't move unless they had something to gain. But Shadi was furious: how could he pay a bribe to receive land the state had already granted? Mohammad smiled. The officials, he said, earned next to nothing. Their survival depended on these little 'sweeteners.'

"Shadi and his friends refused to pay. They kept pushing until they finally managed to get the paperwork through. But when they went to collect the land, they were told there were fees—registration charges: fifty thousand pounds per feddan. God knows how they scraped that together. But they did, in just two weeks. They paid through the post office as they were directed, on the first of May. The land was supposed to be handed over—wells included—immediately. Shadi and Habiba set their wedding date for the end of the year, after they'd finished converting shipping containers into makeshift homes for the group's first two years."

"Then?"

"Then they went to thank the ministers. During the visit, the registration fees came up, by accident. And it turned out that there were none. The whole thing had been a scam. The local team: ministry officials, post office clerk—everyone had all been in on it. The minister exploded. He insisted on prosecuting them—despite the legal advisor, the director general, the sector head all begging him to drop it. 'These are poor people,' they said. 'Their salaries can't even cover a week's costs. What's a few thousand pounds per employee, every few years? That's not real corruption. You'll ruin their lives.'

"But the minister wouldn't budge. He referred them to the public prosecutor. And so it went. The first thing the prosecutor did was release them on bail and suspend the land handover until the legal situation was clarified. That was mid-June 2013."

"And?"

"It's still with the prosecutor's office."

"What about the group? Shadi? Habiba?"

"This was in June 2013, ring a bell?"

"Oh my God."

"Yep."

"Okay. Maybe we should take a break now. Where's Zooba?"

"No, stay. The rest's shorter than you think."

The doorbell rang.

"Thank God for Zooba. Let's eat before the story ruins my appetite. And I need to charge my phone."

"No, get the food and come back. Let's finish the story first."

"As you wish."

She left and returned moments later, then leapt back into bed.

"I put the food on the table. Go on, my lord, I'm all ears."

"When everything happened, Shadi and Habiba ended up in the Rabaa sit-in."

"Wait, why? You said he had doubts about religion. That he was kind of agnostic."

"He went because Habiba went. And because almost all their friends were there."

"So, he just followed her around all the time?"

"What was he supposed to do? Let her go alone?"

"She could've stayed with him."

"That wasn't an option. Habiba was a bulldozer. Once she

believed in something, no one could stop her."

"Not even Shadi?"

"Shadi wouldn't even try."

"So, he followed?"

"What else could he do?"

"I told you he was soft."

"What's this? Where's all this sudden macho talk coming from?"

"It's not that. Just an observation. So why didn't you go?"

"Me? Of course not. Impossible. I know those people. Not just that—when I saw footage of the speeches on the Rabaa stage, I recognized men from my Sudan days—Sheikh Hamza was there! I know better than anyone how deceitful—and dangerous—they are. I decided to go drag my friend out of there. I couldn't let them harm Shadi. I'm no hero. I hate big causes and their champions. I didn't join the January revolution or oppose it or anything that came after. What I know is: you look after the people you know. Your friends. Your family. The ones you can actually help. The rest—grand ideas, narratives about fixing the world—I want nothing to do with them. I've seen how that ends. My father spent his life chasing one of those narratives. Now I'm here—no father, no mother—because of it. Thanks a lot.

"All these people killing each other—in the name of Islam, or patriotism, or social justice. Islam hasn't been lost or spread. The nation hasn't risen or fallen. Social justice hasn't come or gone. All that's happened is that people got killed. As far as I can tell, things happen when their time comes—when the conditions are right—not when people sacrifice their lives, or worse, other people's lives, to make them happen. So, whenever I hear someone calling for sacrifice in the name of a great cause, I say to myself: 'Screw you. Go take care of yourself. Or your kids. Or your neighbors. Do something useful instead of all this nonsense.'

"I felt the same when the revolution broke out. My friends were flying high with joy; I felt only dread—refused to join. I watched the speakers in Tahrir Square, followed every call in the papers and on TV, and said to myself what I always say in such moments. Still, since my friends were in the square, I went with them sometimes. I brought food and blankets for the sit-in at Tahrir and then at every other gathering after, out of friendship and care. Nothing more.

"This was different. This was Sheikh Hamza, who stops at nothing. And the security forces, who stop at nothing. I had to save my friend from the jaws I knew all too well. I went to Rabaa to get him. Shadi was seething after that farce with the farm and the bureaucratic and legal scams. He said nothing would change unless all of it was swept away. Habiba, of course, was even more adamant about the sit-in, about the necessity of 'resistance.'

"I did everything I could to convince them to leave. This was early August. We had a long talk, maybe the longest we ever had. It went nowhere."

"What did you tell them?"

"A lot. Nothing you wouldn't expect."

"I want to know."

"Politics."

"Just tell me."

"I said: 'This is a political sit-in, called for and organized by a political group with political goals. A group that lost power—for whatever reason—and is trying to get it back. And you are tools in that attempt. You are their claws. So, you need to decide whether the return of that group to power, under these conditions, is really what you want.' They laughed at me. They said that what was happening marked the end of all hope—for freedom, for change, for something better. I asked them how they could imagine the Brotherhood returning to power as a good thing, after everything they'd done. We argued about the Brotherhood's rule, their true intentions, who used whom, who rode on whose shoulders, who betrayed whom. Nothing came of it.

"Habiba, with sarcasm, asked if I believed the stories about weapons in the square—the missiles, Katyushas, the anti-aircraft guns. I told them they were armed even without arms. That their very unarmed presence, as civilians, was a weapon no one could match. That those who sent them here knew this. They were pushing them forward precisely because they knew the cost of opening fire on civilians. It was a win-win: either the police couldn't shoot and lost control, or they did shoot and gave their enemies the ultimate weapon—martyrdom. Either way, the movement wins. 'But the price is your lives,' I told them. 'And you know the police will shoot. They don't care about your lives. Behind them are millions who also don't care. Some even hate you.' I told them not to throw themselves away like sheep in a fight between two political camps. 'Neither side is Abraham. Neither has had divine revelation. And you're neither Ishmael nor Isaac. God's not sending down any lambs to save you at the last moment.'

"They laughed, and said I was the lamb, the coward. Habiba said I didn't understand what was happening in the square, didn't understand how ready the protesters were to die. That standing bare-chested before the bullets was the noblest thing they could do. That their blood would stain only the hands of their killers.

"The conversation went on from morning till evening. We left the square, ate, and returned again. In a final effort to convince them, I told them everything about Khartoum, about Sheikh Hamza, the others, my father, the jihadist farm. I told them about the drills, the brainwashing of children, the executions for disobedience. 'Those same men,' I said, 'those killers and rapists are here, in the sit-in. Is this who you want back in power?'

"They shrugged and said there were criminals on every side. They asked me about the killers on the other side—by name. They asked what difference it made. The argument went on. And I could see where it was heading. The old talk of big noble causes. And this time I said it out loud: 'Fuck these big noble causes.'"

"They stayed at the sit-in?"

"They stayed. But on the night before the dispersal, when the leaders began to flee, I went again, this time to drag Shadi out if I had to. I found him shaken, confused. He said he didn't understand what was happening anymore. That he felt like a pawn. That everyone was lying. That the innocent were dying for nothing. That he wanted to leave. Habiba was rattled too. But she dealt with the chaos by doubling down on her principles. She refused to go. She said, 'when everything becomes so muddled, when right and wrong blur, when every idea becomes equally capable of good or evil—then the believer, or the one seeking what's right, has only one path: to do what's right. Not to wallow in endless analysis.'

"She said, 'I'm here because I have a right to be. I'm asking for my rights. No one has the right to attack me for it. It's that simple. Who used whom to achieve what—I no longer know, and I no longer care. I'll stand here alone if I must. Let the army come. Let them kill me—deliberately, accidentally, carelessly—it doesn't matter. God will judge them. The truth will show itself like a white cloth stripped of every stain. No theory, no excuse will save them.'

"I tried again. I told her she was gambling with her life. She said she didn't want life in a society that couldn't tell truth from falsehood—or worse, knew and didn't care. 'That's no life worth living,' she said. 'To die for a belief, a right, a principle—that's a thousand times better than living in rot.' Then she said, 'There's nothing left to say.' And sat still, trembling. Shadi put his arm around her. She broke down and cried against his chest. That's when I knew it was over.

"I was sure Shadi wouldn't leave without her. I left that night planning to return in the morning, to try again to convince her, or drag her out before the crackdown. I went back around the same time the dispersal began. I found Shadi alone, searching for Habiba. He asked me to wait by a small building behind the mosque and went on looking for her.

"He vanished for two full hours. I tried to find him, but the chaos—the tear gas, the smoke, the screams, the bullets from every direction—made searching useless. I went back to the spot where he'd left me. Soon, the bodies began to pass. People carrying corpses, or the wounded—I couldn't tell. At first, they came slowly. Then more. Then, it was a flood. Like I was standing in a river of the dead.

"I followed the stream, trying to see where it led. It brought me to a large room. The bodies went in. None came out. Two men stood at the door, controlling access. They eyed me coldly before I even spoke. I asked, 'Are they dead or wounded?' One said flatly, 'They are martyrs, in God's hands.'

"I asked if they knew who the dead were. One pulled out a bundle of ID cards—clearly snatched from the clothes of the dead. I hesitated, then asked about Shadi and Habiba. The man shifted uncomfortably. He said the women were kept elsewhere, behind another building, which he pointed out.

"Reluctantly, he flipped through the cards. No sign of Shadi's.

"I stood by the door, slowly sinking into disbelief. The whole thing felt like a nightmare. I looked down at my hands now and then, moved my fingers, just to make sure I was awake. I'd seen death before—but not on this scale. Not this arbitrary.

"The flow to the door picked up. I was pushed. I moved with the crowd. I didn't know where I was going. Sometimes people walked as if nothing were happening. I found myself in circles of men or women talking to each other. Then, suddenly, gunfire would erupt from every direction, and we'd all scatter. Sometimes there'd be a body—bleeding, groaning, or just still. Sometimes people picked them up. Sometimes they ran on.

"People were always running. There was always someone shouting.

"Time passed—I don't know how much. I found myself at the door to the room where they kept dead women. I tried to reach it, but the crowd and the screaming made it impossible. I no longer knew where to look. I no longer knew where to go. I was stunned to be there. I thought I was going to die with the Islamists, after everything, after all I'd lived through. I thought about the irony as I gave up, letting the human current carry me. I ran when they ran. Hid when they hid. The gunfire was constant, but I couldn't tell if it was coming toward me or going away. The air was thick with smoke and strange smells.

"Eventually I found myself outside the Square. I stood, dazed, with three others who'd come out behind me. A soldier reached out, grabbed me by the arm, pulled me behind a wall, and pointed—go that way. Then he walked off in the other direction. The four of us walked as he'd said, until we were clear of the camp.

"The next day I learned Shadi had survived. And that Habiba had been killed."

"What misery."

"Yes. But that wasn't the last of it."

"There's more?"

"There is what happened to Shadi afterwards, right before my eyes, without being able to do anything about it. Habiba was killed—no one knows for what crime. She died the way she wanted: laying her blood at the feet of her killers, a weight they'll carry whether they feel it or not. If God exists, they will face Him—He who, as Habiba said, neither forgets nor confuses things.

"But Shadi was still around, except that something in him was gone. It was as if a virus had gotten into him, some kind of malware that kept gnawing at his mind until there was nothing left but the body—still walking but run by the virus.

"The horror he witnessed. Her death. His complete helplessness—that he had been unable to protect her or himself, shattered him. Shattered his pride, his trust in others, his belief in justice or any sense of safety he had in this world. I tried to pull him out of it. I said everything I could think of. But Shadi didn't answer. Most of the time, I don't think he even heard me. I kept visiting him for months. He sat there in silence, like a ghost. And then, one day, he spoke.

"He said, 'There's nothing left to hold on to but power. That was it. Everything else is hot air. This is a country without law, without rules. Nothing protects you. You could be walking down the street and someone—anyone—could stop you and make you do whatever they want, if they have the power. The judge who's supposed to protect you can toss you in prison or send you to the gallows without even looking you in the eye. The officer meant to shield you from criminals can throw you into a cell full of them—to be raped or murdered. The man who feeds you might poison you. The valet might steal your car. It's a jungle, and in the jungle, the only thing that keeps you alive is power. There's no dealing with beasts like this except by force. You live by it. You die by it.' Shadi felt a real hunger to protect himself, and to return the blow. It became an issue of personal revenge.

"I told him I'd heard that line before. Too many times. I heard it from my father. When I once asked him how he went from a lawyer dreaming of change to a sniper jihadi in Afghanistan, he said he came to one conclusion: oppressors understand only force. So, he went after it. But what justice came of that? What did we gain? My father lost his life. I lost mine. So many others lost theirs. So much blood spilled. And nothing, nothing changed. Zero. 'So, what's the point, Shadi?'

"But my words just bounced off Shadi like rain off glass. I told him, 'We have to break this cursed cycle. We can't replay our fathers' script. Even if the oppressors do, we have to be smarter. We have to refuse the part. Don't play the part, Shadi.' He sneered, 'And what do you suggest I do instead? Join the 'Committee to Protect the Democratic Path'?' I told him, 'Even if there's no alternative—do nothing. Disappear. Sleep. But at least avoid the traps we know will destroy us.' I grabbed him, shook him, hugged him—and I never hug anyone—and I wept. For the first and last time. But Shadi wasn't there. He'd already gone."

"Gone where?"

"Toward the fighting, as Fairouz sang, in the far end of the valley.

"The last I heard of him was six months ago. From Mohammed, his father, who returned to Fayoum in grief. He said someone had called—told him not to worry. That Shadi was now in the care of Ansar Beit al-Maqdis in Sinai."

"My God."

"Yep.

"I think the sandwiches have gone cold."

"Maybe. But I'm not hungry anymore. You eat. I'm going to sleep for a bit."

6

Bahaa and Sherif
Flee to New York

Saturday, 3 p.m.

"Awake?"
"Yes."
She turned toward him, suddenly excited:
"Let's go out for lunch."
"Again? Why?"
"I want to go to Left Bank."
"I can't go there."
"Why not?"
"Issues."
"With whom?"
"Two old friends: Bahaa and Sherif."
"That's alright. My friend Ahmed Eid works there—he'll protect you."
"Ahmed's a decent guy, but he can't protect me from memories."
"We don't want protection from memories. Take me there and tell me their story."
"I don't want to leave the apartment. Not even the bed. Wasn't that our agreement? To stay together until flight time?"
"Aren't you bored?"
"Of course I'm bored. But going out is worse. You can go if you want."
"Alone? And what will you do if I go?"
"Sleep, probably."
"Won't you eat?"
"I'll have the cold Zooba sandwiches. Anyway, why would

you go to Left Bank now? It's Saturday—you'll run into everyone you know."

"True...I forgot. Fine, we'll stay. Should I order something else, or are we really going to eat cold sandwiches?"

"Cold sandwiches."

"Fine. I'll get them ready while you prepare yourself to tell the story of Sherif and Randa."

"Sherif and Bahaa."

"Whatever."

Amal inched out of bed and walked toward the living room to the delivery bag. Nine hours left until the flight. The suitcase, the passport, the taxi, Omar, the street, the October Bridge, Salah Salem Road, the airport maze, maybe a few press cameras—she was about to experience all of it for the last time, perhaps forever. She pulled out the food. She hadn't eaten from Zooba in more than a year. The sandwiches were still warm. She placed them on a tray and carried them back to the bed.

"Food in bed? What about the ants?"

"Only nine hours left. How many stories do you have?"

"Plenty. But I don't really have a narrative arc. I tell them as they come."

"Then keep them short. We're running out of time, and I want to hear as many as possible."

"What time do we need to leave for the airport?"

"Around midnight. So, come on. Sherif and Bahaa—what did they do to you?"

"I met them at Left Bank, with Tamer. I used to go there with him a lot, so often that Ahmed Eid knew our orders by heart. I think he warmed to us because we were a bit like him. He had asked where we were from, and when he learned we were from Bein al-Sarayat, he became friendlier—class or tribal solidarity, I guess. Ahmed was decent with everyone, but he was a lot friendlier to us. Left Bank became like our office—we held our business meetings there. When we signed a contract with a big company we couldn't handle alone, we looked for smaller partners and invited them all to Left Bank—that's how we met Sherif and Bahaa. They eventually joined our company and stayed with us until everything unraveled."

"What happened?"

"I don't know where to begin. With their beginnings, with their work with us, or with the end?"

"The end. I don't like suspense."

"OK. Sherif and Bahaa have been in New York for about a year now. They just got their green cards. I don't know how they managed it so quickly, but they have connections, plenty of friends, and they don't hesitate to ask for help. That's what made escape possible."

"Escape?"

"Yes. They fled to New York. Manhattan, to be precise. They live in a small apartment in the Lower East Side. Sherif mocked the name; said he was happy it wasn't the 'Middle East Side.' They have a second-floor flat, with one of those fire escape ladders. They use it as a balcony and drink their coffee there every morning in spring and summer. Bahaa smokes there sometimes too, though his neighbors complained about the smoke drifting into their window. The street is lined with trees; in autumn the leaves turn and cover the pavement in shades of golden yellow and deep red. Sherif posts photos of everything on Facebook: the two of them on the balcony, in the kitchen, in the street, in public gardens, in the subway. In every picture they are either holding hands, embracing, or kissing."

"I see!"

"Yes. The photos have become like a daily ritual for Sherif. Around four in the afternoon here—eight or nine in the morning in New York—there's a new picture of the two of them, in some public place, every single day, weekends included. At first the pictures drew torrents of abuse. But Sherif didn't seem to care. Now I think those who insult them daily have grown accustomed to it, as if it, too, became their ritual."

"And why do they do it?"

"Sherif is the one who posts them. Bahaa closed his account before leaving. I'm not sure he agrees with Sherif's defiance campaign. Sherif makes the pictures public, maybe as payback for all the blows he endured here. He says it's therapeutic, cleansing thirty years of concealment and shame. He told me that when he first arrived in New York, he used to take very long baths, then decided this campaign was a better purification. It's not just about where he puts his dick. It's about reclaiming a part of himself he hid and felt ashamed of for his entire life. He felt guilty for being gay, guilty for his own guilt, guilty for his cowardice and hiding. Thirty years of guilt and repressed anger, at society, at those closest to him, and at himself. A vast load of toxic feelings buried for decades. When he reached New York, he began doing the opposite of what he'd done his entire life."

"But things aren't all shiny in New York, either. There are..."

"Please don't start with nonsensical comparisons," Omar interrupted. "Of course, no place is free of prejudice. But the difference between here and there is fundamental: nothing to compare."

"Calm down, Mister. Bear with me a little. Tell me again: how was the reaction to their social media posts?"

"Reproach, shaming, scolding. Advised to seek therapy, to fear God—the whole thing."

"So, being in Manhattan didn't change much, did it?"

"What do you want? Are you rage-baiting me right now?"

"Just be patient with me a little longer. I'm only asking: why didn't they do this in Cairo? Why the sudden courage in Manhattan? If they were afraid of family shame, of relatives' scorn, what changed?"

"What changed is that they are in Manhattan. Curses from here don't strike them the same way while they are there."

"I don't see why."

"You see only what you want to see. You're locked in your infuriating belief that anything is possible. You don't know how brutal the system is here, how every part of it brings you down."

"I don't know? I am the one who was in jail, you fucker! You, on the other hand, stayed home, unscathed, scrolling timelines on Twitter and Facebook, not bothering to lift yourself from the couch."

"That's not the point."

"What is the point?"

"The point is that you're jumping to conclusions without even hearing the story."

"I told you we're running out of time. Tell the story."

"I will if you stop interrupting."

"I won't say a word."

"Is the phone recording?"

"Ah, now you like the game!"

Omar shook his head in fake despair, and began:

"I first met Sherif when he interviewed for a job with Tamer. Sherif was in his early thirties, polite, single, living with his parents in Mohandessin, working in visual arts. He'd gone to Sa'idiya School, then Cairo University. His family was traditional to the point of cliché, like a TV show: the father a pharmacist, the mother a housewife, one sister, veiled and married. His clothes were ordinary, his looks forgettable. I saw him several times at Left Bank with Tamer and each time I'd forgotten I met him. He was that kind of guy. The project he did for us was a success, so Tamer offered him a job. He accepted with delight—he hadn't had steady work for a while. Bahaa joined a few months later, when we were hiring for a second project.

"Bahaa was different, you couldn't forget him if you tried. He was tall, lean, with deep black eyes, dark-skin, and a smile that drew you in. As you inevitably engaged with him, you'd find him kind, welcoming, quick with a joke, yet also attentive, listened genuinely and always offered to help. He was from Shubra al-Khayma. He went to Cairo University, of course. His father had been a railway worker, retired in 2010. His mother, a housewife. He had three brothers and two sisters, all married but him. The family was desperately poor, but he spoke of it with no shame or bitterness. Once, we were at Left Bank with the team when a girl complained about a piece of fat that came with her steak. Bahaa laughed and said since they could only afford meat once a month, they frequently bought that fat she was throwing away instead: 'to flavor vegetables with the aroma of meat'. She asked innocently, 'What do you eat every day then?' He answered simply, 'Fava beans, potatoes, rice, falafel, or eggplant if the price is right.' When he saw her astonished look, he laughed and changed the subject.

"At university, he sometimes skipped months of school because he couldn't afford the subway fare. Clothes circulated among his siblings, patched and repatched. He also worked after classes—sometimes instead of them. He painted houses, like all his brothers This is how they could afford the once-a-month meat, and the new clothes that fed into the cycle of hand-me-downs.

"Bahaa spoke of it all with a smile. I liked him from the start. He was quick to grasp the potential of social media, one of the first to turn it into a career in marketing and account management. Meat became more frequent at home, and he started to think of moving out, living on his own, but his mother opposed it, so he stayed.

"Strangely, it was Sherif—the reserved one I hardly knew—who told me of their relationship. A week after Bahaa joined our group, Sherif asked me to meet alone, at a café downtown he frequented with his 'friends.' He said there was something troubling his conscience. I grew wary. He told me he had pressed for us to hire Bahaa because of his talent, but there was also something personal he hadn't said. I thought, so what? 'Is he your cousin or something?' He said, 'No, he's my lover.' Just like that. I froze, as if he'd poured a bucket of ice over me, but I kept a neutral face. I was smiling when he began talking, so I kept the same stupid smile. He hadn't told Tamer because he feared he wouldn't understand. But since I was Tamer's business partner, he felt obliged to tell me, to clear his conscience. He asked me not to tell anyone. If I saw Bahaa's hiring as favoritism, I should end it. But if I kept him, I would do so knowing the truth, which eased his conscience. He repeated his plea not to tell Tamer or the others. I nodded, my grin frozen on my face; I consciously changed it slightly from time to time so as not to betray my shock. I then looked at my watch and said I had to leave, awkwardly."

"Why? You have a problem with them being gay?"

"In the abstract, no, it's not my business! But in reality, it unsettled me. My imagination kept conjuring images of their intimacy, scenes I could not help but picture every time I saw them."

"Is that fair? Do you have the same visions when you meet a colleague and her boyfriend?"

"Fair has nothing to do with it. It's simply what was happening in my head."

"Have you ever had such an experience yourself?"

"Me? Absolutely not!"

"Not even in your imagination?"

"Nope."

"Be honest. Remember our agreement."

"I am being perfectly honest."

"Not once? It never crossed your mind? A schoolmate, perhaps, or during those wretched years in the 'North Khartoum farm,' in that loneliness?"

"No."

"And no one ever harassed you?"

"No. Shall I go on with the story, or would you prefer to keep interrogating my sexuality?"

"Go ahead. I feel you're holding something back, though!"

"I tried not to let my unease show. And in time, it faded, I grew used to them, and we became friends like any friends, spending longer hours together, sharing more. Sherif's and Bahaa's life together was hidden beneath the disguise of friendship. Bahaa had made his peace with this. In his view, there was no point in challenging society's deepest fears; no good could come of it. And it wasn't difficult to maintain the pretense. On the contrary, Bahaa insisted, gay couples in Egypt had advantages over heterosexuals: no one ever demanded a marriage certificate before giving them a hotel room. If you accept the necessity of pretense, you'd find the whole thing funny, at worst, awkward, like the time a cleaner walked into their room and found them both naked. Bahaa laughed: 'She was the one who ran away.'

"But Sherif wasn't laughing. He felt hurt, resentful, angry, every time they had to hide who they were. Bahaa would try to lighten the mood with a word, a joke, a change of subject, but nothing worked.

"Sherif's resentment was deeply rooted. His life was marked by a constant struggle with denial: from his first childhood encounter with a boy, through his mother's terrifying warnings, to his attempts to 'cure' himself with a girlfriend. His faith, his yearning for honesty, and his dependence on his mother's approval clashed with the revulsion he felt in forced intimacy with women and the guilt that shadowed his love for men. The result was a life of contradictions—love entangled with sin, authenticity with disguise—where pretense offered safety but felt like a betrayal of both himself and those closest to him.

"Sherif wasn't a revolutionary, but the Tahrir Uprising gave him hope to resolve his dilemma. It turned out that he wasn't alone in wanting a country where people could be free, where their choices were respected, their individuality honored. There were millions like him out there, who had also thought they were alone. And now they all met and discovered they were a community. Since the revolution started, he had been waking up every day asking himself if this outpour of freedom was real, and each day he grew more certain that it was. He wondered whether the protestors would leave the square, whether it would all end that day. But every day they came back, filled the square, and demanded freedom more forcefully, and every day his heart grew warmer.

"It turned out that he hadn't really known this country, hadn't really understood Egyptians. He had closed himself to others, out of fear. He realized how much he had been avoiding people's gaze, in the street, in the subway—everyone had seemed a threat, a potential aggressor. Now he found himself in the middle of a community that was his, of which he was a part. He looked people in the eye, joked with strangers, struck up conversations with them, and smiled. And the more he did that, the wider the world opened, the fuller he felt. That was his description: he said he experienced fullness, and confidence, and strength, and wondered *is this what freedom tastes like?*

"More than once, amid the chants for freedom and dignity in Tahrir Square, he thought of coming out. Weren't all these people demanding freedom and release from the burdens of the past? Didn't that include everybody? Every choice? He almost shouted it out, but something inside stopped him. Not yet. He wasn't ready yet. Even among his comrades in the Square, he saw plenty of repression. Young men scolding girlfriends for their outfits, for speaking up; women expecting men to take care of them, to pay their bills. Young people were shouting for freedom all day, actually risking their lives for it, but they automatically retreated when that freedom clashed with their prejudice.

"He saw all this. It didn't make him love the Square and the revolution any less. It just gave him pause, made him hesitate, ask himself when he heard the chants for freedom: does this freedom really include me, or am I still a pervert in their eyes? He wasn't sure what the answer was. Not yet.

"Instead of shouting it out, he decided to come out to those closest to him. He had no lover at the time, so there was no urgency. But he decided that the time of recognition and acceptance had come, at least for those close to him. So, he began with the closest person to him, the source of unconditional love, his mother. He told her the truth, and she fainted on the spot."

Amal laughed.

"You're right to laugh. Sherif himself laughed when he told me the story. His mother had collapsed from the shock, and when she regained consciousness, she sat speechless, trembling each time he tried to speak, silencing him. She shook her head in disbelief when he explained. Then she ran to her room, shut the door, and avoided him for four days. Then came the tears, then silence again, then attempts to talk, insisting it was a delusion. 'What could you possibly know at twenty?' she asked rhetorically. When he told her he knew very well, she cried out, begged him to stop, and rushed back to her room. Next came threats of damnation, in this world and the next. When he said such threats meant nothing to him, she broke down again, tearful, red-eyed, cheeks swollen, pleading, frightening, and coaxing him all at once. And so it went, a long streak of hysterical days.

"Then one morning, she emerged from her room composed, smiling, behaving utterly normally, as if none of it had happened. She stayed that way all day. Sherif watched her, waiting for the next attack. None came. The following day, the same. And the next. Life seemed to have returned to its old rhythms, until Sherif wondered if he had dreamt it all. So, he asked if she had accepted what he'd told her. She looked at him fondly and asked what he meant. He answered calmly, 'My sexual orientation.' She rebuked him gently, 'Shame on you! This is not a topic for conversation with your mother!' and changed the subject.

"With that, she shut down his coming out plan. If his mother rejected the mere idea, how would the rest react?

"His mother didn't just strike his coming out plan, she dealt a heavier blow to their bond. If the wellspring of unconditional love couldn't take it, how unconditional was it after all? And why would the rest of the family accept him if she didn't? He thought, 'She doesn't love me. She loves her son, her little doll whom she nursed and raised, but not me. And if I want to keep receiving that love, I must keep animating the doll the way she wants. She made that condition explicit.' Sherif grasped his role in that conditional bond of motherhood, and, by the same token, lost his tie to it. From then on, he looked at his mother, and at her doll—the family's 'Engineer Sherif'—from the outside.

"The blow from his mother coincided with the collapse of the revolution. By that time, the Islamists were feeling close to what they thought was their ultimate victory. The tone changed, the language of partnership with liberals receded, making way for emphasis on moral values, religion, and tradition. Sherif felt betrayed, both at home and outside. Where does it stop?

"He decided to test his friends and revolutionary comrades to gauge their commitment to freedom, to see how conditional it was. Most of them failed. Some had clear conditions when it came to women's freedoms, or to the freedom of faith, or to political freedoms, and so on. And nearly everyone recoiled from sexual freedoms, especially when it touched homosexuality.

"Sherif realized that what he had believed to be the sun of freedom, rising in Tahrir Square, had shone only for a fleeting moment, while people stood transfixed, gazing at it. Its rays touched only the sides turned toward it in that instant; each marked according to the angle of their stance. But when they shifted—turning, moving, or merely stirring in place—the hidden sides emerged once more, as dark, damp, and stagnant as it had always been. 'We're back to square one,' he concluded. And so, Sherif basically set aside his emotional and sexual life, directing all his energy to work. That's when he ran into Bahaa, in the job interview. Sherif was instantly drawn, a strong attraction that wasn't just physical.

"Bahaa, too, was drawn to Sherif, and his repeated glances at Sherif gave it away at once—though Sherif, in his usual reserve, averted his eyes. Bahaa understood that reserve as well, he was not put off by it. What did put him off was Sherif's self-centeredness.

"But love is blind as they say, or at least myopic. And Bahaa fell in love with Sherif despite that. He loved his honesty, his compassion, and his loneliness that cried out for rescue. Within a few weeks of working together, of Bahaa's flirting and Sherif's blushing, of late night long texts, their longing overtook whatever reticence they had. And they were both surprised by the speed and depth of their involvement.

"For Sherif this became another chance to reconcile with the outside world. But that required the end of pretense, something Bahaa wasn't quite ready for. At first, Sherif accepted their different perspectives, with some annoyance. With time, the slight annoyance grew, until it exploded in the form of full crisis.

"The crisis erupted on March 22, the day after Mother's Day, when Sherif's mother celebrated her sixtieth birthday. She was particularly affectionate that day, and in the middle of the celebration announced that she had found the perfect bride for her beloved son. Sherif smiled and deflected and later told Bahaa he could not continue living the masquerade. He wanted to come out. Bahaa went quiet. He knew Sherif was serious, it was not the first time he had said this, and he sensed that this time he was more adamant about it. After a pause Bahaa said he was against it, that this was social suicide, that the matter didn't concern the two of them alone but also two sets of families, friends, and an entire society that has a long history of accumulated cultural trash. None of them can be magically whisked away. But Sherif was unmovable. So was Bahaa, who accused him of acting 'like a man,' and asked him to try to see things from someone else's point of view. But Sherif would not listen. The conversation went in circles for hours. By the end of the evening, it became clear to Bahaa that Sherif wouldn't budge; he had one choice; yield or breakup. To breakup would hurt now, but he would survive, and Sherif would understand—eventually. Bahaa thought about it silently, but he didn't want either option.

"There was a third option that Sherif had suggested before: New York. Bahaa had found the idea of leaving Cairo odd back then. How would they even do that? It was not easy to get visas, find work, and settle down in a new country half way around the world! And how would they pay for all that? What would they do in New York, where they didn't know anybody? Sherif's answers had been vague: he had some friends who would help, some money, America was the land of the free, and so on. From time to time he would return to this notion, but they never discussed it seriously.

"Now Bahaa raised this as an alternative. 'It's better to leave then come out, rather than taking this reckless gamble and being forced to leave.' Sherif refused. 'It may be easier, or safer, but it would mean giving up entirely on Egypt.' Bahaa was silent, then after some thought said the opposite was true: if they declared their relationship now, and the reaction forced them to leave, it would mean killing any chance of ever living in Egypt again. They disagreed, went to bed, and the next morning debated it again. That went on for eight days.

"Then, Sherif admitted that what he really wanted was a fight. He wanted to reclaim a self he felt he had lost. Bahaa understood but did not share the sentiment. 'Maybe it's how I am made,' he said, 'maybe I'm more practical, so I don't take all that nonsense personally—other people's opinions don't really matter to me.' When someone mentioned marriage, Bahaa usually replied with a joke and the matter ended there. He had never tried to tell anyone about his sex life, which he also thought was a private matter—not a test to put people through.

"On this issue, he found Sherif both unrealistic and overbearing, but he did not want to lose him. On the eighth night, he made up his mind. He told Sherif that he thought it would be a reckless gamble, totally uncalled for, but he didn't want to abandon him. He would agree but on one condition: they had to prepare for their emigration first; they must have an emergency exit if the situation blew up in their faces. And so they went forward.

"I do not think either of them had anticipated the scale of the fallout. They came out first to their close circle. Sherif wrote three sentences on his Facebook page, restricting visibility to close friends only: 'All love is love. Bahaa and I are together. Freedom of choice is an individual right, regardless of what the majority thinks.' They waited for reactions. None came, for several minutes. Then, private messages trickled into their inboxes, friends seeking clarification. They explained what they meant. That was when the collapse began.

"Some asked whether they were trying to play heroes and embarrass people. Many asked why at this particular moment? Some friends accused them of pulling a political stunt, and a foolish one. They said that in doing this they were serving the Islamists by associating liberal ideas with deviance in the public mind. Sherif replied with something about freedom and its indivisibility. His friends retorted that freedom had limits in every society, and these were its limits in today's Egypt. Some of their gay friends sent panicked messages: 'Why open the gates of hell? Why are you being so selfish?' Some asked if they were 'building a case to seek asylum in America or Europe—

at the expense of those forced to live in this swamp?' and so on. Among the dozens of people they had thought were close friends, only a tiny handful defended their choice. The rest turned on them outright, dismissing them as fame-seekers, glory-hounds, frivolous, even dangerous.

"Sherif flared with rage while Bahaa sank into dejection. Without consulting Bahaa, Sherif took his phone and with two taps changed the post's audience from 'close friends' to 'public.' That was when the real disaster unfolded.

"Bahaa protested when he saw this post, but his outburst lasted barely a minute. In that time an onslaught of comments appeared on Sherif's page, full of 'friends' declaring their shock at Bahaa and Sherif, others regretting having trusted them. Some asked if they had fantasized about them, others wondered if they were child molesters as well. Islamists and their supporters descended on them, by the hundreds, with insults, threats, and dark predictions. Then came hundreds of revolutionary youths disowning them, wondering who had planted them in the revolutionary movement and whether they were agents of the regime. Their announcement quickly turned into yet another battlefield in the country's raging political conflict.

"Bahaa was furious with Sherif. To take such a fateful decision alone reflected either an incredible level of self-centeredness or a complete contempt for Bahaa, or both. His anger was genuine: he told Sherif that under any other circumstances he would have broken up with him over this—but now he couldn't. Sherif, too, grew angry, saying that Bahaa's reaction showed no understanding of the deepest struggles in his life. But they had no time to pursue their argument—a bigger disaster hit them: their families.

"Sherif's sister was the first to call. With an unsteady voice, she told him that his Facebook page had been hacked, and whoever hacked it had posted despicable things in his name. Sherif smiled and told her the page had not been hacked. She fell silent. The silence stretched, then she asked in a broken voice: 'What do you mean it hasn't been hacked? Did you see what's written there?' Sherif answered mechanically that she must be referring to what he had written about his love for Bahaa. Again, silence. Then: 'Yes.' Then more silence. 'But...,' a longer silence. 'Really?' she asked. 'Yes,' he replied. 'Are you insane? What is this? What are you saying?' she pressed him, horrified. He tried to keep calm, answering her gently but firmly. She exploded about the family: had he not thought of his mother, his father, their relatives, their reputation—of her? 'What selfishness! This is a nightmare, you've lost your mind, completely lost it. What happened to you? Damn the revolution and its days, this is what it brought us!' She broke down in sobs and hung up.

"His sister's reaction was a milder version of the responses he received from the rest of the family. His father's was the same in substance but harsher in language and laced with violence—a slap across the face, kind of out of place really, as if the father had felt an obligation to do it. Then, in a melodramatic tone, he declared that Sherif was no son of his, and he would never recognize him as one 'unless he renounced this nonsense, claimed his page had been hacked, and shut down that damned 'Facecrap' entirely.' Then he added that Sherif should seek treatment for this perversion and definitively put an end to it. The rest of Sherif's relatives simply disappeared; none called, none spoke. They simply vanished from his page and his life.

"But, of course, the most important reaction came from his mother, who said nothing at all. She just seemed to have aged suddenly, her face frozen in a permanent grimace. She did not call; Sherif went to see her. Half an hour after he arrived, she came out of her room, eyes glassy. She asked about his work, whether he was eating well, about his apartment and if he kept it clean. Then nothing. When he told her he wanted to speak about a delicate subject, she rose, saying she was too weary for delicate subjects, patted his shoulder with something like affection, and went back to her room.

"Bahaa's family's reaction was far simpler. They summoned him to the house, and when he arrived, he found them all waiting. One of his brothers asked if what his 'friend' had written on Facebook was true. Bahaa nodded, ashamed. His three brothers leapt on him, beating him until their father ordered them to stop, leaving Bahaa crumpled on the floor, bruises on his face, arms, and right leg. The father spat on him and left. His eldest brother told him he was 'expelled from the house, forbidden to return, to call, even to set foot in Shubra al-Khaymah again.' If he did, they would 'rid themselves of him forever.' Then, he threw a bag of Bahaa's clothes in his face and ordered him to leave at once. Through it all, the mother hid her face in her headscarf, perhaps weeping silently.

"And, of course, there was the campaign of support for Sherif and Bahaa. Strangers they had never met took it upon themselves to defend their right to choose: #Rights, #StandWithBahaaAndSherif, etc. Famous bloggers, revolutionary youth leaders, writers, and journalists joined in. Many asked to meet them in order to show their solidarity. At first, they agreed. Some celebrities came, posed for photos with them, posted them instantly, then disappeared, leaving only the occasional comment to repeat the same slogans.

"Their professional lives collapsed quickly. My cousin Tamer fired them, despite my objections. Sherif suggested they start their own firm, focus on clients outside Egypt. Bahaa said nothing. He was too angry at Sherif.

"Sherif and Bahaa had expected most of these reactions—though not the opportunistic 'solidarity campaign.' But expectation is one thing, the lived experience another. It is easy to say: 'My family will boycott me,' or 'They will disown me.' But to have it actually happen! To feel that silence, that chill, that estrangement from one's mother! The intensity of it shocked them, as did the sharp pain it brought. They had not expected this, had not expected the reactions to wound them so deeply. More than that, they felt no relief in their coming out. Even Sherif, who thought of this as his life's struggle, found no solace in coming out. On the contrary, his sense of isolation and discomfort only deepened. These were the feelings that had consumed him in his years of pretense; he had imagined that coming out would end them. Instead, it merely released them into the open, scattering them around him, until he felt them pressing in on every side—on Facebook, at work, and in the streets. Neither of them had ever been part of the underground 'gay community.' And now they belonged to no community at all. Everywhere they went, silence wrapped their lives, like a wet blanket.

"Once, they went to Left Bank, and when they walked through the door the place truly fell silent. Almost everyone there knew them and hushed at their entrance; the rest fell silent in surprise at the sudden hush. Our mutual friend Ahmed Eid was kind as ever, taking their order, bringing it with a plate of fruit as a gift. But the tension in the room overwhelmed them. After a few minutes Bahaa said he could not stay. Sherif paid, and they left, ignoring Ahmed Eid's polite protests.

"The silence weighed heavily on their life. But when the greater disaster struck, they missed the silence terribly. One evening, as they sat in their apartment after returning from work, at exactly ten o'clock, someone pounded violently on the door. They were about to break it down, and Bahaa went to see who it was. When he opened, two men shoved him aside, and several others poured in—including some of their neighbors. Sherif and Bahaa were arrested and taken to the police station, to be brought before the prosecutor the following morning. And of course, what one expects in an Egyptian police station did indeed happen. They were not raped, mercifully, but they were beaten and humiliated in every other way. Photos of them on their way to the station spread online, followed by others showing them half-naked, likely after being stripped and beaten inside the station. By morning they were delivered to the prosecutor and charged with multiple offenses: debauchery, perversion, lewd acts, and incitement thereto.

"The prosecutor was sympathetic. He said he had no interest in this nonsense, but their neighbors and landlord had filed a report at the station. The police officer had been reluctant to act, but the landlord and the neighbors threatened to storm the apartment themselves and deal with Sherif and Bahaa in their own way. The officer informed the prosecutor, and they both decided arrest was the lesser evil.

"The newspapers filled with stories of the case, with their photos. Sherif and Bahaa were shattered—by the arrest, by what they endured in custody, by the 'investigation' itself, the medical examination, the stories circulating in the media, the neighbors with whom they had been on excellent terms a week before, everything.

"Fortunately, some human rights groups picked up their case the very night they were arrested and sent lawyers to assist them. The prosecutor agreed to release them on bail pending trial and hinted to their lawyer to handle matters as he saw fit in the meantime. The lawyer gave them the keys to his own flat, where they stayed. He went to their apartment to collect clothes and belongings the police had not seized or destroyed—their passports above all. The next day they bought two tickets to New York on separate airlines. The day after that, they left Egypt for New York, never to return."

"They were lucky to escape!"

"Bahaa never wanted to leave, not even at the last moment. And I think he is unhappy there, despite Sherif's attempts to suggest otherwise. But the lawyer told them, 'If you want to run, this is the time, before the case grows larger and the sympathetic prosecutor is forced to ban your travel or jail you pending trial.'"

"Bravo for the lawyer, and the prosecutor!"

"Do you understand now? Don't you see there is no hope? That the problem is not only the state; that people themselves are hopeless?"

"I'm exhausted. Why is it so dark? What time is it?"

"Six o'clock."

"Let me close my eyes for a bit."

7

Dina and Ayman
at the Appropriate Limits

Saturday, 7:30 p.m.

"Awake?"
She asked.
"Yes."
"What are you thinking about?"
"Nothing."
"How can you think about nothing?"
He turned toward her.
"What do you want?"
"Nothing."
"How can you want nothing?"
"Nice try! But it is true. I want nothing."
"I don't believe you."
"What do you think I want?"
"I think you want to stay."
She laughed. "Yes, I love you and I want to stay with you forever."
"I didn't say that."
They were both silent for a moment. Amal sighed and changed the subject, "Are you worried about your father?"
"Yes."
"Do you really think he won't come back?"
"Yes."
"Why?"
"I think he's able to come back if he wants to. But I believe he wants to finish what he started, there in the desert where it

began."

"And what will you do? Is there a way to communicate with him?"

"We had one, and we lost it."

"Really? Who?

"Dina, Colonel Ayman's wife."

"You know her?"

"Aunt Layla knew her when my father was driving the taxi. Dina got to know the whole family then, and she and Layla got close. But then things happened, and they cut off ties."

"What things?"

"It is a long, sad story."

"Do you have any story that isn't?"

"Not really."

"Alright, hold on, I'll start recording again. Do you have a USB?"

"I don't."

"I think I have one in my bag. Wait."

She got up, then returned with her phone and a flash drive and motioned for him to begin.

"So, tell me about this cat fight between Layla and Dina."

"There was never a cat fight; it was rather a conjugal fight."

"Was it because of Layla?"

"Because of Layla, Fakhreddine, me and the whole situation."

"Because of your father's imprisonment?"

"No. Because of love."

"The plot thickens. Pray, tell. I'm all ears, my lord."

"Yes, my lady, at your service. Dina is a gentle, soft-spoken woman. She is refined, but also practical. She was thirty-five when she had her daughter, Injy. Her childbirth had been difficult, and afterward the doctor cautioned her against trying again. Ayman wanted a son, but the doctor warned him that such an attempt might leave him raising Injy without her mother, so he backed off. Dina is the daughter of the former undersecretary of the Ministry of Agriculture. Her mother is a housewife with a BA in Art History. Dina had a brother and a sister who moved to the Gulf decades ago; they appear in the summers with their children, and the family gathers in a chalet on the North Coast that Ayman rents through his work and Dina hosts her parents, brother, and sister there for a week. Ayman was usually absent from these gatherings; he would show up at the beginning or the end but avoided most of it. It was an unspoken agreement between them that she would have that time alone with her family.

"Like her mother, Dina chose to care for husband, child, and house instead of working. Although it wasn't entirely her choice. She had actually wanted to work, had started working after graduation, but Ayman convinced her to give it up during the engagement. 'You won't need to work,' he would insist 'Build us a happy home instead, a nest.' 'You can do whatever work you want, but without the constraints of an office and competition,' and other nonsense men tell women to dissuade them from working. As a child, Dina was a dutiful girl. She learned to appreciate the importance of family, children, and awaited the day she would become a wife—a full woman, reigning over a home that would be her kingdom, with a man and child she could be completely devoted to. Don't assume from this that she was reclusive. Not at all. Dina was lively, eager for life, joy, and freedom—but within the appropriate limits.

"These limits made Ayman a perfect husband. He was of an appropriate age, with an appropriate job; he was handsome, courteous, and strong. He liked her liveliness, which contrasted with his strict upbringing and promised new horizons for his life with her. He wanted her to help him unshackle himself and enjoy life, 'within the appropriate limits,' he added. She found herself echoing the same phrase. They laughed, and the phrase became one of their inside jokes. As Dina came with promises of joy and freedom; Ayman came with promises of stability and safety. They had a beautiful daughter they named Injy, likely because of their repeated viewings of *Return My Heart.*

"Yet disagreements appeared from the first day of marriage. They resembled each other outwardly, in their insistence on minding the 'appropriate limits,' but they saw almost everything differently. She was religious like him, but he thought her freer than necessary in her way of thinking, her desires, even in their intimacy. She felt he was more reserved than necessary, in behavior, thought, and speech. Sometimes she called him old, a relic of a generation past.

"Once married, he plunged into work. His job was important and required irregular hours. To him, it was more than a job, it was an integral part of who he was and how he related to his family, friends, neighbors—everyone. Being a police officer didn't just stop when he left the station, it shaped his entire life. Even more so because he worked in State Security. Dina understood the importance of his work and accepted its unique requirements. In fact, she liked it—the safety and social standing it gave her. Their arguments were never about his work, but about something harder to grasp. They disagreed on life, on their role in it, on what was right and what was not. It seemed theoretical at the beginning, but it reflected itself in practical issues a lot. Ayman didn't know how to handle it, and his mother—his adviser on the affairs of women—wasn't much help, either. So, they kept arguing about this and that, and the disagreements grew, little by little, especially as Injy grew up.

"Yet, their domestic life went on unperturbed, as it often does in such cases. They were neither fully content, nor wholly unhappy. Each of them tried to steer matters their way and did their best to avoid clashes; they tried to let go of what seemed minor, and to have patience in bigger things. But eventually they would collide; usually it would start with a conflict over Injy or an offhand comment about the other's character, and the argument would grow into a dispute. They defended themselves, explained their position, questioned each other, and the argument would always end up with at least one side feeling wounded, wronged, and misunderstood. After the argument, each would retreat and be tormented with worries that they had wasted life with the wrong person, with thoughts of divorce and its potential toll on Injy and on each other's standing in society. These thoughts would inevitably end in general misery and fatigue, followed by sleeping in separate beds. In the morning, Ayman would leave early without seeing her, and if they did happen to run into each other in the kitchen or bathroom, it was often silent. By the end of the day, though, they would reconcile—one would receive a text about something practical, then another, then a kind word or a small gesture, maybe a joke, and things flowed back again. And if he came home early and had some energy left, they would have sex and bury the previous day's argument.

"Day after day, month after month, year after year, they learned to respect the boundaries that separated them. They accepted the division of their life into two zones and abandoned the fantasy of completely sharing it. Now and then they clashed across the borderline, privately mourned what might have been had they chosen someone else as a partner. Certain parts of them continued to hope that change might someday come. Until my Aunt Layla arrived."

"Oh, I was just about to enjoy the tale!"

"Sorry! This happened months after the revolution started, in October 2011. Fakhreddine, my illustrious father, had been sentenced to prison in January. Ayman put him there and forgot about him in the midst of the revolutionary upheavals. Layla was also swept up in the revolution, but obviously in a different way. Poor Aunt, she thought the old regime had fallen, so she hurried to draw the new regime's attention to the injustice inflicted on Fakhreddine. She sent petitions, letters, and appeals to the ruling Military Council and the new government, explaining his story and the injustice he suffered, and urging his swift release. She met youth coalition leaders, members of the new parties, journalists and so on. She appeared on national TV to recount his story, her eyes watering as the camera projected her crying face across the screen. She wrote dozens of Facebook posts that thousands liked and hundreds shared; the hashtag #FreeFakhreddine topped Twitter for two days. The Interior Ministry spokesman announced that the Ministry was studying his case thoroughly; revolutionaries protested that the Interior Ministry had no say, since Fakhreddine was already sentenced, and it should be in the judiciary's hands. The public prosecutor mumbled something about reviewing the case too. Then the whole thing faded out, drowned under the weight of hundred other issues that flared and died that year.

"By October, Layla understood that this path would not free Fakhreddine. She wanted to knock on Ayman's door directly. But Fakhreddine suggested a little plot. He had written his memoirs, and gave the manuscript to his friend Fishere, together with an old report about his disappearance in 1987 that had been written by a prosecutor named Omar Fares.

"Fishere the novelist you mentioned earlier?"

"Yeah, the 'novelist.' Fakhreddine asked Layla to tell Fishere to publish both documents as 'novels,' which he did. There was only a limited number of copies, but it was essential to make these documents into some kind of fiction. Layla took a copy of each 'novel' and gave them to Dina, Ayman's wife, and told her what their real source was."

"Why did she do all that?"

"These 'novels' included almost all the details of Fakhreddine's story. This way, Ayman would know everything he wanted to know, would understand how Fakhreddine was the victim in the story. If he sympathized with my father's cause, if he realized that he had been acting in good faith despite his breaches of the law, then he would help him. If Ayman remained captive to his old mindset, the knowledge would change nothing; but he would still lack legally binding evidence to back it up—just a couple of mediocre novels!"

"Wait, and these novels are available? Like I can find them online?"

"Kind of. One is available only in Arabic, called *Killing Fakhreddine,* the other is available in English as well, called *The Egyptian Assassin* or something like that.

"That's so cool!"

"Whatever. My father was wrong to expect Ayman's sympathy. Ayman was going through the hardest time of his life and his appetite for cooperation was nil. He was suspended himself, awaiting trial. Ironically, he was charged with something he didn't do. He was in his office the day protestors stormed the State Security headquarters. He was shredding documents, as instructed, when they broke in.

"Like many of his colleagues, Ayman worked from home after that, most of the time. Sometimes he went to some unknown offices in the Ministry of the Interior. But the incident had scarred him: how had it come to this? How had they lost control to that point? The people he used to round up were now in control, and he and his colleagues—the ones who actually protected the state - were forced to hide?! To him, this was literally the world upside down. But Ayman had no alternative, so he kept working in these strange circumstances, hoping things would change. And they did change, but for the worse. One day, he found himself referred to court, charged with destroying State Security documents!

"Picture it: you do your job, rather well, you monitor and apprehend terrorists, and one day while you're in your own office, some of those terrorists storm in. So, you take the proper steps to protect the office and the documents according to protocol. And somehow that lands you in court, accused of destroying evidence. You, who had spent your entire life sending people to court for breaking the rules. Naturally, Ayman protested, asked his superiors for an explanation. They told him the protestors had identified him, and they couldn't cover him. He asked what right the protestors had to judge the police. They shook their heads and said the world had turned upside down. His colleagues told him not to worry, and to go along with it, to buy time until God opened a way. He had no real choice: the same agency that now handed him to court was the only source of power he ever had.

"Thus, when Dina appeared at the door of the room that had become his home office, carrying two novels and saying they contained the complete story of Fakhreddine Essa, he exploded. His anger wasn't directed at Dina alone, nor at Layla, nor even at Fakhreddine, though all three of their names were entangled with his insults. His fury was aimed at everything that had happened and was happening to him since the damned revolution started.

"Dina had never seen this side of him. She was more terrified by his rage than hurt by the unusually cruel insults he threw at her. He seemed to have turned into someone else who only resembled her husband, like the 'Hulk'—but red, not green. What truly shook her was the fear she felt as she stood before him, not knowing where his anger might carry him. For the first time, she felt unsafe around him: suddenly realizing he was capable of anything—hitting her, perhaps worse. Questions she had avoided for years forced themselves upon her: was her husband—the handsome, polite, attentive, tender man—capable of real harm? The kind of harm she had read about, heard about, seen in films? The red man standing before her, pounding things with his fists, shouting without pause, strong enough to lift her and hurl her out the window if he chose, that man, what exactly did he do in his secretive job? What did he do with the real villains, the terrorists who carried weapons, bombed, and slaughtered people? What did her husband do to them when they fell into his hands?

"Her reaction startled him. She stood there, calm but absent, as if she had slipped somewhere else, stepped outside the scene, leaving only her body there. Even in the midst of his rage, he realized something in her had 'switched off.' That was enough to remind him that the person before him was Dina—his life partner, the mother of Injy—not some protestor scaling the agency's walls, or an activist shouting against him in court, or a former terrorist smearing his reputation on television.

"Gradually, he calmed down, realizing that his rage had perhaps caused serious damage. He, too, fell silent, then moved to self-pity, hoping it would erase the image she had just witnessed. He sat down and buried his head in his hands, muttering things about his misery, the injustice done to him, his wasted career, the country's threatened future, his sense of impotence—his inability to protect the country or even his family—and how men like Fakhreddine were behind all this.

"Dina remained silent. After a moment, she said all she had done was take two novels from the cousin of his own former driver, or the man he had said was his driver! Novels containing stories, not bombs. She said she was sorry to upset him that much, but she couldn't have guessed that delivering two books could cause all this. Ayman reminded her of the instructions he had given her since their marriage: never to touch his work. She said she remembered, and that she had never once gone near it, even though the entire country had been discussing it for months. She paused, then added that his reaction was unexpected, excessive, and frightening. Then, she placed the two books on his desk and walked out.

"Dina remained shaken for days, and Ayman's reconciliation attempts failed. She did not cut him off: she spoke with him, carried out her domestic duties, but avoided his gaze. She went to sleep before him or long after, leaving him no chance to touch her. When he reached for her in the middle of the night, she stiffened, then shifted away just enough to escape his touch. The estrangement lasted longer than usual. Gradually, Ayman realized that something had broken down. That this momentary appearance of the 'red man' had done something to her sense of safety. And, therefore, he had to do something equally unusual to mend the fracture.

"He came home and rang the bell instead of using his key. When she opened the door, he hugged her. She stiffened but he kept holding her and apologizing. He didn't try to offer justification, just apologized profusely. He told her that his life was worthless without her, that he was worthless without her, and that all he wanted was her approval. He said he was deeply sorry for hurting her, that he never intended to, that his fury had not been directed at her but at the terrorist who had infiltrated his home. She replied that no terrorist had infiltrated their house, only two books, passed from one grieving woman to another. Ayman smiled, saying that no terrorist was worth making her upset, that he admits he was in the wrong, completely, and ready for penance. She asked what he meant, he said he was ready to read the books aloud if that would please her. Dina smiled for the first time in a week, telling him she wanted no part in his work. He answered that this was not work, he was suspended anyway, and if she wished, they could read the novels together, every night, like watching a TV series. He even offered to get an additional copy of each so they could read it simultaneously.

"Dina was shocked. She knew his usual tricks—pleading, clowning, desperate persistence—but this was new. Pretty smart, she thought, and couldn't help a wide smile, which he seized upon to kiss her, passionately. The matter ended as it should, in bed, with the couple reconciled and content—Ayman was more attentive to her than usual, and succeeded in making her come, for the first time in a long time. A full reconciliation.

"He had not been joking about the reading, either. He actually got another copy of the novels Layla had brought. Dina prepared a light supper—sandwiches, a pot of tea, some fruit—and they settled in the living room to read. It was a wholly new scene for her, 'seems like the revolution has finally made it to my home,' she later told Layla.

"The two novels complemented each other, as Layla had said. They began with *Killing Fakhreddine,* the report by Omar Fares, the prosecutor who had taken five years' unpaid leave to track down Fakhreddine's story from its beginning to what he described as its 'end.' The novel contained a mixture of interviews the prosecutor had conducted and tales he collected from a variety of sources—some of them realistic, others bordering on fantasy. There was a sheikh who appears and vanishes, stories of Fakhreddine dying multiple times, that sort of thing. There were also scraps in Fakhreddine's handwriting from different periods of his life, and writings by his friends. Ayman dismissed the novel as mere fiction, but he had promised Dina, and he would keep his word. They agreed to pause after each chapter to discuss a little. They finished the introduction quickly. Ayman quipped about a prosecutor abandoning his post for the trivial case of a missing young lawyer: 'If everyone did that, we'd have no prosecutors left.' Dina gave him a reproachful look, and they read on. Over time, Ayman's sarcastic remarks dwindled, his expression darkened; Dina, too, fell silent, lost in the pages.

"Neither kept their agreement. When Dina finished the first chapter, her eyes were brimming with tears, and she saw Ayman absorbed in reading, so she continued. Ayman was taken aback: though he hated Fakhreddine, the prosecutor, and everyone linked to this chaos, the novel contained an astonishing amount of detail about Fakhreddine—details which, if true, explained much of that terrorist's behavior. From time to time, he shook his head in wonder, sometimes in anger, and sometimes muttered a curse or two, usually at Fakhreddine. After nearly an hour, he rose, fetched his laptop, opened a file and kept it by his side, consulting it now and then as he read. Dina was submerged in silence, occasionally slipping out to the bathroom and returning with a washed face, until she brought a box of tissues and set it beside her.

"Just after 1 a.m., Dina folded the book, set it aside, and sat staring blankly. Soon Ayman finished as well. Holding the novel, he said in a low voice 'This is unbelievable; it contains the entire Fakhreddine case, naming everyone he killed. Everyone mentioned here was murdered!' He had spent months combing through Fakhreddine's file at the agency, and all this information was sitting there, in some amateurish novel, published! Who was Omar Fares? Why did the prosecution's archives have no trace of him? It was clear to him that Fishere was just a façade, a ghost writer; the question was how did the original report end up in the hands of Fakhreddine?

"Dina was drowning in her empathy for Fakhreddine, while Ayman was boiling. 'This chaos is what led us here,' he murmured. Dina tried to turn the discussion away from his security concerns, pointing to the tragic sides of the story—and there are many. Ayman was unmoved. He couldn't get over the severe negligence surrounding the case from the start, 'The seed of rebellion was obvious, so why didn't anyone address it? Why wasn't he court-martialed when he defied orders during his military service? Why wasn't he held accountable for any of his repeated transgressions?' Dina argued, 'Were these really transgressions or just a young man coming of age?' 'Coming of age?' cried Ayman indignantly.

They went over every story of Fakhreddine's, his military service, his love life, his work, his years in college, with Dina trying to explain how a rebellious, free young spirit would run against all these established and rigid rules, 'most of them, let's face it, are hypocritical.' Ayman rebutted her arguments. Unsurprisingly, their divergent assessments increasingly reflected their own disagreements. As this became painfully clear, Dina said, 'It's late, I'm going to bed.' Ayman was too angry to argue anymore, so he just nodded. He wished her good night and said he would continue reading for a while.

"The story of Fakhreddine not only exposed the rift between Dina and Ayman; it tore open the wound inside her. She had chosen the safety of marriage to Ayman over passion. She had thought, back then, that following passion was a folly. Her friends and mother had told her so. She had told herself so. Even Mahmoud, the object of her old passion, had said it.

"Mahmoud understood her better than anyone. If she had chosen him, had followed her heart, she would have spent her life feeling bitter about the safety and stability she would have missed. He loved her, but he understood that love wouldn't be enough for her, so he let her go while she still loved him. 'Better,' he thought, 'to love and miss me than to stay and be miserable and sour.' He knew that ultimately Dina would choose safety—it was more important than love, even though love was sweeter.

"Safety was indeed important to her. With Ayman she would never fear for her children's needs, never fear for her standing among family or friends. She would always be respected, sheltered, and taken care of. Who would refuse such a deal? She had chosen it, and she got what she chose, and life went on fine, more or less. But when she read the story of Fakhreddine, especially the details of his own love story, and the story of his cousin Layla, the missing sweetness of love hit her like a wound reopened. Fakhreddine had done the opposite. He had followed his passion and faced daunting challenges and consequences for it—but he lived it. Layla, his cousin, had settled for similar reasons to Dina, and ended up losing both passion and safety. Was she making the same mistake? Had she wasted her life? And where was safety now, with her husband awaiting trial?

"Ayman felt no sympathy for Fakhreddine's tragedies. He was not a cruel man, only pragmatic. His job wasn't to fix the world, it was to protect the state, and he would not let anyone undermine it. Fakhreddine's idealism infuriated him, not because he disliked the ideals, but because he couldn't stomach Fakhreddine's deception and defiance. He couldn't swallow the fact that all these mysterious crimes that he had failed to resolve for all those years were carried out by this man, right under his nose. Not only that, but this murderer, this deliberate and focused terrorist had managed to win his trust enough to become his family's driver. He had let him drive his wife, his daughter, and his mother. Fakhreddine made a complete mockery of law and order, and of him personally, and that was not something Ayman could forgive, no matter what ideals once animated Fakhreddine.

"Dina's sympathy for this terrorist enraged him. It gave flesh to something elusive in her; something that had always annoyed him but slipped away whenever he tried to pin it down. A soft spot that she seemed to have for people who make mistakes, a tendency to find excuses for all sorts of weaknesses and misbehavior. He had told himself it was harmless kindness. But it wasn't. It was almost a fondness of weakness of character, of disorder. Now he understood; she hated rules, she belonged to the other camp: she was like Fakhreddine, like the protestors who stormed his office. She was one of those irresponsible cowards. She wanted to hold on to dreamy ideals, while he and his colleagues shouldered the burden of hard choices to protect her life, only to be chastised by her and her likes.

"Now he understood why she had been cool toward his work all those years. She had never condemned it openly but never praised it or took pride in it either. She was never enthusiastic about it, never really cared for his success, only vaguely, as if he were a civil engineer and not an officer who put his life on the line every day. She had been lukewarm when he succeeded in rounding up an important cell or organization and always found excuses for those crazy fools. 'Almost a sleeper cell herself,' he thought. The only redeeming factor was that she did not know she was one. If she had not been married to him, she would have probably been sleeping in tents in Tahrir Square, or co-renting one of those squalid downtown apartments with a bunch of activists. Ayman drew a long breath, smothered the thought, and ended the day.

"The next morning, the couple resumed their reading, this time of Fakhreddine's own memoirs—published in Arabic as *Abo Omar El-Masry*. It was effectively the second part of Omar Fares's report *Killing Fakhreddine*. Here, Fakhreddine gave a full account of his story, explaining how he had transformed from a dreamy and idealistic failed lawyer into a professional killer at the hands of his friends in the jihad organization, first in their camps in Sudan, then in the mountains of Afghanistan, then back in Egypt where he took revenge on all those who had wronged him. Ayman was livid with rage: at his wife who cleared her throat occasionally at the end of the room, thinking he did not notice her stifled tears, at Fakhreddine, with his relentless crimes and his attempts to justify murder and terrorism, and at himself.

"Ayman tried to focus, first things first. He now had a full account of the crimes Fakhreddine had committed since his return to Egypt, up until his escape to Sudan to save his son from his fellow Jihadis. He also had the story of Fakhreddine's comrade in terror—Sheikh Hamza, who had returned to Egypt after January 2011 and wreaked havoc across the country. He had the answers to the questions he had failed to extract from Fakhreddine, from the files, from other agencies. Yes, this was a novel, not evidence, but Fakhreddine was still in prison. The important thing now was to settle that matter once and for all.

"He rose from his chair and told Dina curtly that he was going to his office. He gave her a stern look when she brought up Friday plans with their daughter. He dressed and left, asking himself why Fakhreddine sent him those novels? Did he imagine that Ayman could sympathize with him, help him? Or was there another purpose? Clearly, Fakhreddine didn't do anything without ulterior motive, so in what direction was Fakhreddine trying to push him now? Ayman sent someone to fetch Fishere for questioning, but he knew that wouldn't get him anything useful. The only person who could give him useful answers was in prison. He decided to go there and confront his nemesis; to get all the information he needed out of him. Ayman didn't have a clear plan, yet, but he was determined on one thing: that Fakhreddine would never leave the prison alive.

"The problem is, when Ayman came home that evening, Dina was gone.

"On the dining table, there was a note. In it, Dina said that she could no longer live this cold life, she had tried to live without passion but could not go on. She asked for divorce. 'This cold life?' 'Passion?' 'Divorce?' Ayman wondered if this was the result of the damned story she had read, or whether she was upset about something else. And what passion? Had he been neglecting her? Did he ever refuse her something she wanted? Was this a ploy, did she want something big, and this was a prelude to extracting his approval? Was she pregnant and this was some hormonal shit? 'What happened to that bitch?'

"He spent the following days doing what any reasonable husband would: trying to calm Dina down, appease her, reconcile with her. Then he began pressing her: 'Our only daughter,' 'your family, my family, people,' 'the future.' Then he interrogated her: 'Was there another man, someone in her life, even in her imagination?' 'Had she been with someone before their marriage?' 'Did she love another?' 'Had she cheated on him?' But none of these tactics worked. Pressure did not move her. She would not yield, would not soften. She met his provocations and accusations only with calm, confident scorn. He pleaded with her to be reasonable, then swore that he would never divorce her, and threatened that she would see a side of him she had never known. Her father, Mr. Mustafa the Undersecretary of the Ministry of Agriculture, took his side. But nothing worked. Then Ayman left her parents' house, asking them to talk sense into her, while they both nodded in agreement.

"Dina herself did not know what she was doing. Had anyone told her a day earlier that she would leave her husband and her home, she would have laughed in disbelief. What had come over her? Was it that cursed novel? Could Dina truly leave? And why would she leave now? For whom? Mahmoud had been the only one she loved, and she had not been able to marry him. And that was years ago, when she was young. And she had known from the start their love could not be built into a life. She had known it before he did, then made him see it. He did, and accepted the outcome, out of care; he would not bind her to a life of bitterness. He had left without rancor, and she had cherished him for it. The love endured, and even now his name did unsettle her heart a little. But what did that mean? Would she leave Ayman and seek him out? Why would it work now, even if he were free, even if Ayman released her?

"And what about Injy, her daughter? How could she tear her from her father, bring another man into her life? Ayman would never allow it. And who said Mahmoud would want her? Who said their life together would be better? These were illusions, she told herself—cheap echoes of films and novels. What she needed was a bucket of ice over her head, to collect herself and go home. But the thought of returning gripped her with dread. So, she fell silent, staying at her parents' house, waiting for her mind to clear.

"But her mind did not clear. The longer she stayed, the larger the thought grew, until she felt paralyzed. When Ayman came, she recoiled; when he insisted on entering her room, she froze, like a stone. His anger turned to fury, then to worry. Had she gone mad? Her mother advised him to step back, give her time, and he did. But he hated it. He hated his empty house, hated life without his wife and daughter. Yet again, Ayman was pragmatic and made what seemed to be his best available choice. Dina needed time, so be it. He retreated, camped in his office, and focused on saving his professional life.

"As Ayman and his specter receded, Dina collected herself and her thoughts. Old friends appeared, mostly summoned by her mother. None could help, except for one, who urged her to find Mahmoud. Which she eventually did, with that friend's help. First a few messages, then a call, then a videocall.

"He was the same, almost. Divorced, with a son, and still in love with her. He worked as a cinematographer. 'When did you learn filmmaking?' she asked. 'I don't know. But this is what I became.' He made documentaries featuring Cairo's streets, graffiti, youth, the pulse of the city. His income was modest, his life chaotic: cafés, bars, his old neighborhood, artist friends. He looked like the Tahrir crowd: his clothes, his hair, his way of speaking Her friend pushed her, 'Try. It's better than spending your life wondering what would have been.'

"Dina wanted to, but couldn't, until she did. They met once, and then again, then in his home. They kissed, then they gave in to their repressed passion, and soon it became an ongoing thing. Twice a week she slipped away under the pretense of visiting her friend and spent the day with Mahmoud.

"Her life brightened. Colors returned, sounds grew sharp again. She became a gentler mother, more patient, more loving with her daughter, a kinder daughter to her own parents. Her mother noticed, understood, and said nothing, for Dina's sake, for her granddaughter's, even for the sake of her marriage to Ayman. She guessed where all this would end and chose silence. Dina must not know she knew. No one must know. That was best for everyone.

"Dina didn't notice her mother's recognition, she was intoxicated with love, with passion, with life. Then, came the thought: *what now?* Her answer developed through multiple stages. The first stage, lasting about a month, was spent with Mahmoud in the fever of planning her divorce from Ayman, their marriage, a new life.

"The second stage, which lasted another month, was when Dina discovered—though Mahmoud denied it—the immense difficulties shadowing the plan. Beyond Ayman, beyond the child, there was Dina herself: her expectations of marriage, the shape of a life with Mahmoud who had not changed from the man she had left years before.

"She thought of returning to Ayman and keeping Mahmoud as a lover. But a marital affair is a complicated business, demanding skill and nerve, and she had neither. And cheating on a State Security officer was a bit risky. So, she concluded that this wasn't a real option for her. She told herself she was not cheating yet: she was separated from Ayman, probing her limits. But to return and live with him under one roof and constantly lie to his face—that she neither could nor wished to do.

"The third stage, another month, was when her life with Mahmoud drowned in the ordinary. The initial rush ebbed, habit crept in, and his flaws grew visible. He irritated her a little; she irritated him, too. The magic didn't disappear, but it thinned. And the arguments began. So, Dina asked herself in the plainest terms: would she gamble her stability, her daughter's emotional life, for another marriage that in the end might resemble the one she already had? Maybe with fewer benefits? Wasn't every marriage a sum of gains and losses, joys and resentments? Mahmoud would make her happy in some ways, unhappy in others. But the total—hers, her daughter's, her family's—would probably remain unchanged, or maybe less. The math was merciless. And so, she ended her non-affair, first while in her mother's house, then returned to her husband's.

"Ayman opened the door, not out of forgiveness but pragmatism. He was tired of the empty house, of the office couch, of the glances—mocking, pitying, curious—of colleagues and superiors. He wanted his household back in order, a semblance of normalcy. If Dina had erred, he, too, had not been blameless. Their daughter was growing, and he would not want her to grow without him. He opened the door and let Dina in, with her silence, her melancholy, her brittle smile. He opened the door and chose, for his part, to endure. Something remained in the air between them, dividing them even in the same rooms, but they ignored it, concentrating on the child, on routine, on avoiding conflict. And so that she would not again sink into gloom or restless thoughts, he arranged her a post in the office of some minister."

"You know you're a real son of a bitch!" Amal derided.

"Great! Finally, you spoke your mind!"

"And a gloomy one. Even the love story you invented, you made as bleak as your dark soul!"

"Invented? Who said I invented it?"

"Surely Dina didn't tell you the details of her feelings, her cheating on the State Security officer who jailed your father."

"True, she didn't tell me. But she told much of it to Layla, my aunt. And besides, it's common knowledge she left Ayman and then returned. Even if some details came from my imagination, do you see anything in the story that doesn't make sense?"

"The issue isn't whether it makes sense. All your stories are plausible. But they can go in wholly different directions. The problem is you're dark, and you cast that darkness onto the stories!"

"All right, Miss Positivity. Next time, you tell your own stories!"

"OK, Mr. Gloom. It's nine o'clock. Let me nap for half an hour."

8

Amal and Omar
Reach the Edge of the Bed

Saturday, 10 p.m.

"Awake?"

"Yes, you?"

"Awake. What time is it?" She turned toward him.

"Ten."

"We still have two hours."

"Then let's sleep some more."

"You want to sleep till the very last moment?"

"I want to sleep until these shitty days are over."

"The shitty days won't end as long as you keep sleeping."

"We're back to the theoretical stuff again."

"And what's the practical talk, then?"

"That in two hours I'll drive you to the airport. I'll stop at the terminal gate while you go through security, check in, then go through immigration. The officer will give you a look—a mix of hatred and envy—as he stamps your blue passport. Then, you'll cross the line between shit and life, step into a plane that takes you out of this swamp, while I remain stuck in it. So, what do you want from me?"

"I want one last story."

"I'm done with stories!"

"No. There's still one left."

"Which?"

"Ours."

"Ours? Now we have a story?"

"You tell me. You're the storyteller. You're Scheherazade."

"If we have a story, it's a very short one."

169

"Everyone knows the length doesn't matter, it is the effect."

"I like how positive you always are."

"I like how gloomy you always are."

"Don't you get tired of it?"

"Don't *you* get tired of it?"

"You're funny," he smirked.

"I don't see you laughing."

"I laugh on the inside."

"Fine. Stop that and tell me our story."

"I don't know that story. Why don't you tell it? You seem to have a clearer idea. Go on."

"Alright, let each of us tell the story as we see it. I'll start, since you're stalling. But come here to bed first. Lie next to me. No, I don't want to have sex—I'm exhausted. I just want to feel you beside me."

"What's this? Love?"

"Just come here and be quiet. I'll tell our story."

"OK."

"Listen. First, I'll send you a friend request on Facebook. How do you spell your name?"

"Omar Fakhreddine. But my account's private. I don't accept requests."

"Cut the nonsense. I'll send it and you'll accept."

"How do you spell yours? I couldn't find it when I looked."

"Amal Mofeed. Instead of snooping, wouldn't it be better to drop the pathetic secrecy, accept some friends, and show yourself like the rest of us?"

"Tell the story."

"Alright. Tonight, I'll fly out of here. We'll stay in touch, and then I'll send for you to join me. You'll come to the US in a month, and we'll rent a two-bedroom in DC. Egypt will vanish from our lives for a while, and we'll just be a boy and a girl trying to live. At first, you'll be lost, unsettled, asking yourself why you came. We'll live like roommates, no emotions, no special bond. I'll see other men. You'll pretend you're fine, but you'll be annoyed. Questions you never knew existed will start hounding you. You'll grow insanely jealous, hate yourself for it, but never admit it. Then, you won't be able to stand it. You'll take a job, any job, just to have income and move out—you'll be a bartender, perhaps. It would suit you. But your pay won't cover living alone, so you'll stay with me, reluctantly. Then, you'll start seeking revenge. You'll bring home women, one after another, a new one every week. I'll feel disgust, repulsion—and intense jealousy will consume me. I'll feel diminished. After a while, humiliated, I'll strike back. I'll confuse you, seduce then reject you—deliberate torture. I'll show you how beautiful, attractive, tender, clever, and capable I am—and how deprived you are of it all, with no way to have it. Memories of these two days in bed will swell in your mind until they explode. The girls you bring home will all be substitutes, but poor ones. The more you sleep with them, the emptier you'll feel. Until you collapse completely."

"Wow. You thought this plot through! Then what, you'll catch me?"

"Not necessarily. More likely I'll have lost interest by then. I'll tell you to move out. I'll keep saying that I consider you a friend, a brother. And I'll believe it. Then you'll leave, share a dingy apartment with some guy, and we'll each carry on—having feelings for each other without knowing how to be together."

"Brilliant. You've caught the bug for happy endings."

"Don't rush. We'll go on like that for a year or two, each of us earnestly involved with someone else, thinking it's love. Then we'll leave them, one after the other. And then we'll come back to each other, on new ground, as equals, knowing ourselves better, seeing each other for real, not as a reflection of who we wanted to see."

"And we'll marry and live happily ever after?"

"No, we won't marry. But we'll live happily ever after. Each of us will become a better human being. I'll practice law, become a good lawyer, maybe specialize in cases I care about—public interest or class actions against big companies. Maybe I'll team up with lawyers from different countries and create an international legal defense group, quiet and efficient, no fuss, achieving modest but decisive victories. And you—you'll go back to school. Or rather, you'll start school. You'll discover how smart you are. Your professors will find you gifted and help you. You'll study something computer-related: graphics, design. You'll do it for months, then grumble that the market is ahead of the university and quit. But since you have a scholarship, you'll take other classes—writing, world history, psychology—in hopes of untying your knots. I'll encourage you. While you keep working in design—maybe with your gay friends, Sherif and Bahaa—you'll lean more and more into psychology, until you graduate, train, and become a therapist. Then you'll write a book in Arabic on child psychology. Non-academic. It'll spread through the Arab world like wildfire. Overnight you'll become a star. But because you're grounded, you won't lose your mind. You'll tour the Arab world, including Egypt, then return to Washington. You'll leave design behind and focus on therapy. You'll write a second book, which will fail miserably. No one will read it. They'll say it's just a repeat of the first, or a cash-in, or that you've lost your spark. Something deflating. But because you're grounded, you won't break. You'll carry on."

"And what about us?"

"We'll stay together for years, at least seven."

"Without marriage?"

"Of course."

"Without children?"

"Of course. I don't want children. I don't want to be a mother. And you don't want to be a father. We'll agree on that. But I'll get pregnant once, by mistake. That will be our biggest crisis. I'll hesitate about what to do. When I decide to end it, you'll hesitate. Both times we'll fight. But we will end it—together, and we'll remain sad for a while. Now and then one of us will say something about the child who would have been our child's age, if we hadn't ended it. The words will hurt. But we won't try again."

"And we'll live in America forever?"

"You will. I'll return to Egypt. At first just for a short visit, just to annoy the authorities. You'll come later, also just a visit, after getting your U.S. passport. Then I'll decide to return to Egypt and live there for a while."

"Really? You'll go back?"

"Of course. I'll go back to set up a training institute for lawyers."

"Foreign funding?"

"Exactly. But this time Egypt will have woken from its madness, begun to stand on its feet again."

"Inshallah."

"Well, we'll disagree on this. You'll say my optimism is nothing but naivety or stupidity. You'll refuse to come, will stay in Virginia—in the little house we bought together—while I return to Egypt."

"And then?"

"Then, we'll part. Quietly. Not only because of physical distance, but because our paths will pull us apart. I'll be more and more immersed in life here, in building a new state still in formation, which will mean plunging into politics. You'll go further into psychology and writing. You'll write in English after your third book in Arabic, which will be very successful. You'll become a serious scholar, maybe a professor. You'll stay emotionally tied to Egypt and the Arab world—but from afar. Something like Edward Said."

"Edward Said? Shouldn't I at least enroll in college first?"

"You will. And you'll excel. For the record, Edward Said wasn't a stellar student. His academic interests came late."

"Alright. And how will we part?"

"As I said: quietly. Our parting won't be bitter. There will be a wistfulness to it, like watching a child grow into adolescence—still the same but transformed. We won't formally separate until I ask for it. I'll write you a long letter, explaining my decision, telling you I met someone in Egypt and fell in love, asking for separation."

"Why would we need a formal separation if we were never married?"

"Don't be foolish. What binds us will be greater than formal marriage. I couldn't move past it without a mutual acknowledgment. You'll agree, gently, sadly. We'll separate. I'll marry this man and have his child."

"And who's the lucky man?"

"An Egyptian I'll meet when I return, maybe at a party like the one you were at two nights ago. Maybe his name is Omar. Maybe it's you—the one who refused to travel and stayed here!"

"Clever. Nice. I think we need a break. Want something to drink?"

"Water, please."

Omar got up to head to the kitchen, but she pulled him back. He hesitated, not sure what she intended. Amal knew he was searching her face for a clue, trying to understand what she wanted him to do, and decided to toy with him a little. She drew him close to her face as if to kiss him, then pulled back, placing his head on her neck and holding him. As he tried to wrap his arms around her, though, she broke free, pushing him away. He stared at her, baffled, and she smiled. Her behavior only deepened his confusion, and irritation flickered across his face. She ran her fingers across the tension in his features, smiling.

"Go on, bring me the water."

Omar sighed, impatient but good-natured, and rose again from the bed. She tugged at his arm again, but this time he slipped from her hand and went to the kitchen. Darkness gathered through the house. Omar returned from the hallway carrying two small bottles of water; he gave her one and took a sip from the other. She studied him closely until, finally, he asked curtly:

"Is there something interesting about the way I drink water?"

"No. But there is something interesting about you."

"What?"

"You don't know what you want. Despite your harsh experiences, you still don't know what you want. Or you do, but you look for what others want to decide how you'll act."

"Mashallah. We have a therapist already!"

"Not at all. Just an observation. Never mind, go on, your turn for the story."

"Whatever. Like I said, if we have a story, it would be short."

"And sad, of course."

"Shut up. It's my turn. Listen. You will send me an invitation to join you in America. But I won't go. State Security won't let me travel. And even if they did, what about the family my father left for me? And what would I do in America, with what qualifications? What life awaits me there? And above all, what would I do with you? Just because we spent two days in bed doesn't mean we could walk a hundred meters together outside this door. True, I've never had days like these before, but bed isn't life."

"Who told you that nonsense?"

"Shut up, please. For all these reasons I'll dismiss the idea. I'll answer your generous invitation with an explanation. You won't like it. You'll try to persuade me. I'll refuse, firmly. The only outcome of this correspondence is that State Security will summon me—because they monitor everyone you contact. The interrogation will be humiliating, or harsh, or both. It will bring out the worst in me. I'll clash with Colonel Ayman, or whoever replaces him after he dies in the desert with my father. I'll end up in prison, pending some made-up charge: drug possession, assaulting a soldier at a military-run gas station, stealing an armored vehicle, harassing a submarine— something like that. Either my case will drag on for years in the courts while I rot in 'pre-trial detention,' or they'll try me in a military court and give me five, six years."

"I knew your story would shine."

"You'll defend me from over there. You'll hire lawyers, launch some campaign—#FreeOmar or #NoMilitaryTrials— and maybe get some American official to demand my release. But since I'm a nobody, and have a history they can use against me, none of that will matter. I'll stay in prison day after day, filling with boredom and bitterness. And when I finally get out, I won't be fit for anything. You'll have 'returned,' as you put it, and you'll meet me, but we won't love each other. We won't even sleep together. I'll have lost the desire, along with whatever else in me was still alive. After the first rush, driven by memories, you'll realize we're two different people, with nothing left to say to each other. We'll part, without a second meeting. If someone asks you who I was, you'll mumble: 'Someone I met during my first stay,' and move on with your life. And I'll go back to floating in my own bitterness and boredom."

"You're a real bundle of joy. My God. Excuse me, I'll just throw myself out the window and be right back."

Amal rose and went to the window, opening the pane. The air felt cold on her face. She remained there for a moment, breathing, then turned to see him staring intently at her. She smiled, teasing, but he said seriously, "Time's ticking. Your flight is getting close."

Amal returned to the bed. She sat next to Omar, pulled him closer, looked into his eyes filling hers, and whispered, "Tell me, how can you be this sweet and this bleak at the same time?"

"Look where I live, do the math. What kind of human being could I be under these conditions?"

"You're so much more mature than any twenty-two-year-old guy I've ever met. So why does that maturity stop at analyzing the disaster? Why can't you push past it? Are you a bot? Can't you resist circumstances? Are you stupid, or do you see some kind of beauty in wallowing in misery?"

"And what, exactly, should I do?"

"Learn something useful, for yourself, for humanity. Make yourself an expert in something, anything. Pick a field you like, any activity, transporting fruits and vegetables, teaching children, plumbing, anything, and master it until you understand it better than anyone. Everything in this country is collapsing. That means any expertise in any field will be valuable. One day, at some point, someone will need it, and then you'll be there."

"Sweetheart! The guy who built websites got arrested. The one who recorded a song got arrested. The one who helped street kids got arrested. The one who tweeted got arrested. The one who wore the wrong T-shirt got arrested. We're all under arrest, we live inside a detention center!"

"Then do something you can't be arrested for. Gain some kind of skill."

"As if there's a shortage of experts! Think of all those old men with PhDs and decades of experience, experts in everything from nuclear physics to literature—and none of them are capable of anything. The moment one of them gets a post, he turns into the same idiot as the one before him. What use are the experts? Haven't you figured out yet that the problem isn't lack of expertise, that it's much bigger than that? Didn't this stay in prison teach you enough?"

"Of course there's a bigger problem. But there's also ignorance and lack of expertise. Very few people know how to solve this country's problems. Get out of your shell, out of your grumbling and depression. Look around and learn about the place you live in—how to fix the crookedness that's crushing you. You mock me for being a foreigner, but the real foreigner is you. You live here, but what do you actually know about the lives of people here—outside your family, your friends, and what you hear? Do you really know them?"

"Of course."

"No, you don't. You haven't the faintest idea. Didn't you say Ahmed Eid is your friend? Ask him."

"Ask him what?"

"Ask him about his struggles, about the people around him. Judge for yourself whether you know people. Half of Egypt lives under the poverty line. How many of them do you know? Go, discover the country you live in. Travel with Ahmed to his village and see how people live in ruins. Try to learn a way to fix even a sliver of it. Everyone dreams, everyone has demands, but no one knows how to make them happen. When you figure out a way to ease some of the burdens of Ahmed Eid's people, you'll find a way out of your own despair."

"Sure. I'll do that and join the President's Youth Initiative."

"There we go again, back to empty sarcasm."

"Stop the nonsense, Amal. Stop imagining that willpower can beat reality. Don't you get it? There's no point in doing anything on a sinking ship. We're on the fucking Titanic, we've already hit the iceberg, a quarter of the ship is underwater, and you want me to tidy a corner of the deck!"

"Do you really, honestly believe there's no hope? Not even a glimmer? Isn't that why you're still here—or is it just because you're fond of the food?"

"I did have hope, for a short while, a few months, maybe. Right after the revolution started. I, the one who believes nothing, believed. Quietly, without telling anyone, I let myself believe. And that's the problem; I believed, against my better judgement. Then events piled on, and my hope turned into an even greater disappointment. Hope is a painful illusion. There will always be people like you, telling people like me about some ray of hope under the rubble, ok? The harsh truth is that the rubble is larger, heavier than the fucking ray of hope. The rubble is inside people themselves, enough rubble to crush any hope they might carry. This isn't emotion, it's a cold reading of reality. Plenty of societies have collapsed, disappeared, or became marginal, dependent, paralyzed, or rotten. Those ruined countries also wanted to live, to grow, to prosper. But wanting is one thing, ability is another. As the American saying goes: 'you can't beat something with nothing.' And here—we have nothing to beat with. Everything is diseased, rotten, and broken, including us. The people themselves are broken, incapable."

"I completely disagree with you."

"Good for you. Actually, I've even lost interest, not just hope. Why should anyone fight to fix a country when those in charge of it don't want it fixed? If they're happy with themselves, who am I to object? I'm not their guardian. And that idea of selfless sacrifice, this martyrdom syndrome is ridiculous. The martyrs of the revolution: we'll die so you can live better. No one lives better unless they act to improve things, and this requires cooperation, from everyone. Everyone! Do you understand? For this country to climb out of the pit it's fallen into, everyone has to work together. And that's simply impossible. If we could, we wouldn't be here."

"If that's what you believe, then why not leave? Why not come with me?"

"As I told you. State Security told my father they won't let me leave Egypt. Even if they did, what about my aunt and the rest of the family my father left behind?"

"And what are you doing for them now? Sleeping beside them?"

"I take care of my aunt. Her health won't allow her to live alone."

"You live with her?"

"No, she lives with my Aunt Layla."

"So?"

"So I help them both. I can't leave them on their own."

"And where is Tamer? Isn't Tamer enough?"

"Tamer just got out of prison. He's angry. Shattered."

"So are you."

"You don't understand."

"Clearly. What you're saying is nonsense. Is there a woman involved?"

"What woman?"

"I don't know. You mentioned a girl you used to love."

"What girl?"

"Stop repeating my questions. You said you went to the workshop because a girl you loved dragged you there."

"Oh, her. I don't know where she is. We lost touch years ago. I haven't heard from her since. She vanished."

"Just like that? Didn't you love her?"

"I don't know. Maybe. We dated for a while, then split up. She said I was depressing, and she worried she'd catch it. We didn't have much in common. She dragged me to workshops, meetings, things like that. I always said it was a waste of time. We'd argue, then we stopped arguing, and she did her thing without me. We stopped seeing each other."

"And you? Did you do your thing without her?"

"Yeah."

"And what's your thing?"

"Not much. Spending time with my friends—those still alive, free, able to speak. Or watching people."

"You mean observing?"

"More or less."

"Observing life?"

"Observing everything."

"But why not take part in life yourself? That's what I don't get. Don't you want to do anything?"

"As I told you: 'The only use of shitty days is sleep.' And these are shitty days. So, there's nothing to do but sleep. I'll sleep, waiting for something to happen."

"And if nothing happens?"

"Then time will have passed."

"Aren't you afraid of rotting from so much sleep?"

"Afraid of rotting? Everything you see around you is rotting. That's exactly what I've been trying to tell you: we've rotted, all of us, with our revolution, our counter-revolution, our quarrels and disagreements. We've been rotting slowly, and we go on rotting with spectacular success."

"And this position of yours doesn't strike you as defeatist, as surrender?"

"Only on the surface. The truth is, just getting through time is a huge victory."

"Why?"

"Oh, you're exhausting! You should have been a prosecutor! Because the world is harsher and more painful than I can endure. If it weren't for fear, I'd have ended it long ago."

"Then, thank fear."

"Don't rely on it too much. Fear has a way of weakening, sometimes."

"Don't do that. Please don't do that."

"I'll try."

"The apartment's gone dark. Want me to turn on the light?"

"It doesn't make a difference to me."

Amal returned to bed with a steaming cup. She sat back against the headboard and sipped slowly. Omar lay awake on his side, his back to her. Without turning his head, he asked:

"And you? What will you do?"

"I don't know. I agree with you that these are shitty days. But I can't just sleep. I'm twenty-nine, and I don't want to sleep now—maybe when I'm sixty. But I don't know what to do with myself, or where to go, until these shitty days are over. I'll go back to the US, that's certain. I'll stay there, or maybe go to Europe, but will stay in the developed world. I won't go to any developing country anytime soon, nor to any dictatorship. I'll stay in the upper half of the planet for a while. I need to recharge my humanity: learn new things, nurture my soul. I want to excel in something, though I don't yet know what. Sometimes I think all these trips to developing countries were just me searching for that thing. But it was a search in the wrong place, in the wrong conditions.

"Here, this is my confession. It was easy to feel special in my position, working in the fields I worked in. I could tell myself, 'I'm helping a nation rise—me, Amal Mofeed, in my twenties, a freshly graduated lawyer, with a modest family background, and nothing making me special except being entrusted by donors to manage their money.' Of course that makes one feel special: sitting at the money tap, deciding which idea gets life and which becomes nothing. Everyone comes to you, because you can grant or deny. Naturally you feel special, exceptional even. And it's easy to turn that into a permanent status: make it a career, move from one organization to another, one country to another—becoming more important and more 'special' with time.

"Prison was time to reflect, to measure my real size, stripped of the pretenses my job had bestowed. Endless hours of nothing, sitting alone, awake, through whole nights. I don't think I've ever felt time the way I did in prison. Imagine having all your tasks and distractions stripped away, left only with food, a bathroom, and sleep, alone. How many hours in a day, how many minutes, seconds, thoughts crossing your mind, pricking you, scaring you, haunting you?

"Prison gave rise to all sorts of questions. 'You did what you did, girl: you came from the far end of the earth to help Egypt. You, in your twenties, became important, effective, challenged an authoritarian state, walked into prison with your head high to teach them a lesson, to show them their mistake. Bravo. And then? Who are you really? Beyond the silly question of whether you're American or Egyptian, who am I, as a person? What am I doing, not just here in this miserable cell, not just in this wretched country, but generally, in life? What am I doing here? What is my role, or do I even have a role? What are my limits?'

"I had a usual answer to this line of questions: I was a human being, and my role was to help the less fortunate, to clean the place if it was dirty, to extend a hand to the drowning so they may float. That, I always thought, is what it meant to be human. But the truth suddenly seemed more complicated. Without my US citizenship, without my job, I am nothing but an average lawyer—one who has never even worked in a courtroom. Stripped of pretenses and privilege, I was nothing. Nothing sets me apart. I excel at nothing. Nothing that makes me unique. I saw this, and I did not like it. I loathed the false glitter that covered me all this time, and all this media attention like I was some kind of superwoman. I do not want it. Any of it. Not anymore. This is a bubble—it does not fill me, it imprisons me. And I want to get out. But I don't yet know what it means to be out, or where that is."

"And how will you know?"

"Not sure. I need some rest first, I need the world around me, and inside me, to calm down a bit. A break."

"You need to sleep!"

"Yeah, right! And there's another confession."

"What?"

"I thought a lot today about what you said yesterday, after Hend and Bassem's story"

"What did I say?"

"That my ideas are abstract, arrogant, detached from reality. That I have the luxury to think this way because I feel permanently shielded."

"Yes."

"I thought of this as you told me your wretched stories. And I think you are partly right, but not entirely."

"How so?"

"My sense of protection, the strength it gives me, allows me to rise above the painful reality and look at it from outside.

Even in prison I was calm. I felt the humiliation and degradation of prison life, the filth, the waiting for the guard's permission for anything you need—going to the bathroom, getting medicine. I felt all that, just like the other prisoners. But I was always calmer than them. And soon they stopped speaking to me, because my detachment annoyed them. This detachment, this calm, would have been impossible without the sense of protection I had, without knowing with certainty that I would get out. That feeling overwhelmed me all week since my release. I kind of won. I am here, free and famous, carrying my US passport, my ticket, and they had to release me. Everything feels lighter, I kind of feel invincible. And it is not unrelated to the protection I have."

"Hallelujah!"

"Wait."

"What?"

"That doesn't make what I said wrong or make what you said about my ignorance of Egypt's conditions right. Once more, I am not a tourist, I know this country as you do, maybe better. I feel it, it touches me. I am no spectator. But I can take a step back and see Egypt from outside, as a spectator. And I think this is probably what you need to do, if you want to cope with life here and find a positive way to engage with it."

"And how can I do that without the protection you enjoy? How, knowing that Ayman is on my ass and can throw me in prison at any moment—me and my entire family?"

"You can, if you find a point outside all this to anchor your gaze. If you find your own 'America.'"

"And what might that be?"

"You want me to answer, so you can mock me? No, you must find it yourself."

"Please. I have no strength to think. I promise not to reply."

"Fine. Don't reply. Just think."

"I promise."

"Your true protection, the anchor beyond this madness, your 'America,' is simply your understanding, your conviction, that all this nonsense is temporary. That all this shit around you is going extinct. That these decrepit men cannot suppress an entire country forever. They are simply doomed, no doubt about it. And all you must do is prepare yourself for what comes after—for the moment when you are free of their grasp, for that moment when they collapse, which they will."

"I'll keep my promise and not reply."

"That's a good start. Think, not about the triviality or nonsense of my words, but search them for some small fragment of validity, perhaps. And if you conclude that I am wholly wrong, that there is no hope for life in this country, then leave it. Just decide to leave. Send for me and I will find a way to get you out, even if I must marry you."

"Still not replying."

"Bravo."

"And what will you do about your case against the Egyptian government?"

"I'll sue their ass. I'll give it to a law firm and let them handle it while I take a break from it all. I need to cleanse myself of what has seeped in over the past six years, from the revolution, the martyrs and the dead, the torture victims and the eyes of their families, the lies, deceit, stupidity, baseness, cruelty. I need time to drain out the poison that has entered my soul here. And I need better things to nourish myself with—things to replace that shit, to carry me somewhere better. I don't know yet. I'll know in time. Step by step."

"And Chris?"

"Oh, you remembered his name! Yes, Chris. That will be the first case I deal with. It's more complicated than it looks. Our marriage has been dead for a while—not because love died, but because circumstances changed. The truth I have been avoiding is that there was no love to begin with. What was there was something else, what we politely call 'companionship.' That wore away with time. We blamed marriage, life in Egypt, his constant travel, or whatever. But the truth is our marriage was based on convenience. We married because it was practically useful for us both. And I knew I was compromising. The funny thing is that I didn't really have to. I had no family pressuring me, no friends besieging me with their children, no society driving me into it. I chose it freely."

"What compromise? I don't understand."

"A compromise of my right to love. I was always very particular about who to marry and when, if ever. But I suddenly gave up. Chris was an easy, convenient arrangement: a kind, calm, and sensible man in the middle of a madhouse. Marriage made it easier to deal with people. It made them place me in a safe category, which I badly needed after months of constant harassment. It also made life easier in practical terms. It was convenient for him too—he gained legal residency, a comfortable home. Marriage to an Egyptian, or half-Egyptian, partner opened doors and helped his work. My sister asked me whether this was really the man I wanted, whether marriage that quickly and under such circumstances was wise. I told myself I was marrying 'for Egypt,' so I could focus on what mattered more. It was pure arrogance, a delusion that my work here was more important than my personal life. The truth is: nothing is more important than personal life. That is real life. The rest is words.

"And I think I knew it, deep down. Sometimes I asked myself about the difference between this arrangement and someone marrying—or sleeping with—a man for money. I asked myself this when he laid his hands on me, and I knew I couldn't push them away again, and ended up having sex out of duty—as part of the arrangement I had accepted. I evaded the question, brushed it aside as an unfit thought. Until finally we stopped sleeping together. And so it went. Of course, he began seeing other women. He never said it, but I knew. And I, too, had my little flings on the side. Our marriage became a mere arrangement: a shared house, a budget, mutual obligations, a social front. That is why I snapped when you called me a *sharmoota*, because I think I did act like one. Not by sleeping with you, but by sleeping with my 'husband.'"

"I'm sorry! I didn't mean to upset you!"

"That's the first time you've apologized. You know, in prison I came to understand how life here pushes people to strange extremes. It's like madness is contagious. Like being in a carnival, you're thrown into unnatural acts that you'd never commit elsewhere. Anyway, nothing is left between me and Chris. We both know it. No hostility, just remnants of friendship, and a wish to move on without each other. If not for all that happened, we would have divorced long ago. But the case and the prison made it harder. I think we'll file for divorce as soon as I arrive."

Omar smiled without replying. He rose from the bed and walked to the bathroom. On the way he glanced at the wall clock. Eleven o'clock. Almost time to leave. *What a pity,* he thought. Was he falling for her? No, certainly not. Besides, he didn't even know for sure what love was. But she was no ordinary woman, of that he was certain. He had never met anyone like her. She understood, she was curious—asking questions and listening, truly listening. And she was completely open. She stripped him of his usual defenses: she was neither submissive nor controlling; she didn't play games. Sincere. That was the word he was looking for—sincere, genuine. She was both strong and weak, without posturing. And she was beautiful, and warm, and at ease with her body and his. Certainly, if she stayed in Cairo, he would have loved to keep seeing her.

But this isn't love, he told himself. *Then what is it?* he wondered, sitting on the toilet seat. Friendship? No. She filled him, cleared his body and soul and thoughts, as if recharging him. He wanted a woman like her, or her. So, what to call this? He had no label for it. Are labels necessary? Who needs them? Then he laughed at himself: who needs all these questions? She was flying out tonight, now. Still. Then, secretly, as if whispering in his own mind: *Why not leave with her?* 'What nonsense! Where would you go, to what life? You're staying here, this is your place, your swamp.' *But why not?* 'Why not! Do you really ask that? Didn't you hear yourself giving her the answer?' *But isn't there at least a chance it could work, if you went with her, followed her?* 'No, not a flicker of hope. Not a snowball's chance in hell, as the Americans say. Don't give in to illusions, not again! Enough folly. And who would even let you leave? Back to bed, you've half an hour left. Maybe one last time with her, if you still have the strength.'

***

Amal got up first. She looked at Omar and found him asleep. They had come together, quickly, then dozed off together. *The boy must be worn out,* she thought as she leaned over him with a kiss, stroking his hair. Startled, his body jerked. She smiled.

"Easy now."

"Is it time?" he asked.

"Yes."

"What time is it?"

"Twelve."

"Yes, we have to leave now. I'll take the bags down."

Omar dressed quickly. Amal went to the bathroom and returned in jeans and a gray jacket, wearing another coat over it, a scarf on her shoulder. Omar carried the bags to the door. Amal went through the rooms to check nothing was left behind, slipped a few small items into her handbag, and stood by the door. Omar came back in to find her standing just behind him.

"You've taken everything?"

"Yes. There are some cigarettes left. Do you want them?"

"Sure. To remember you with."

She buttoned her coat, wrapped the scarf around her neck. She looked at him and smiled; he smiled back. Then they hugged, awkwardly. Amal held on, until he pulled away, smiling.

"You'll be late."

"I transferred the audio file onto the flash drive. You have it, right?"

"Yes."

"Will you give it to Fishere or put it online?"

"I'll see."

"As you like. Anyway, I have a copy. If you don't, I'll send it to him myself."

"Fine."

"And will you keep me posted about your father?"

"Yes. Let's go."

"Tell me first: will you think about what I said?"

"I will."

"And will you do something useful with your life?"

"I doubt it."

"Will you follow me then?"

"No."

"What will you do then?"

"Most likely, sleep."

ALSO BY EZZEDINE C. FISHERE

Embrace on Brooklyn Bridge
(translated by John Peate)

The Egyptian Assassin
(translated by Jonathan Wright)

Exit
(translated by Jonathan Smolin)

ABOUT THE AUTHOR

Ezzedine C. Fishere is an Egyptian-American novelist whose work explores the intersections of politics, identity, and everyday life in the modern Middle East. He is the author of nine novels, three nominated for the Arabic Booker (the International Prize for Arabic Fiction), with two adapted into acclaimed television dramas. A former diplomat in Cairo, Jerusalem, and Khartoum, he was a prominent voice of the Tahrir Uprising before moving to the United States in 2016. He now teaches Middle Eastern politics at Dartmouth College.

www.ingramcontent.com/pod-product-compliance
Lightning Source LLC
Chambersburg PA
CBHW031041160726
47991CB00005B/1985